CU00869127

Cimone O'Byrne

Children of the Periapt:
Escape from Elmsmere

Cover Illustration by Eleanor Loseby

DEDICATION

This book is dedicated to my wonderfully, fantastical family and friends. Every, last one of them. A special mention goes to my beautiful children, Dotty and Jonah. They are the inspiration for every word I write.

Contents

Chapter 1: Elmsmere Academy

Vinnie Shadowsmith stared up at the tall, wooden doors of Elmsmere Academy as they loomed over him. Closing his eyes, he took a deep breath and choked back the fear lodged in his throat. Drenched in their shadow, he looked down from the doors and wallowed in his dampened spirit. Sensing the heavy hand of the Seeker on his shoulder, he shuddered. He puffed out his chest and raised his chin. If he was going to go into this place, he was going in with his head held high.

The door creaked open and five tiny fingers reached around the thick, polished wood. A small, round face peeked through the gap.

"Ah hello, hello there. We weren't expecting you today. Come in, come in." The door flew open and Vinnie was pushed reluctantly forwards.

The woman who opened the door was short and stout, with silver hair tied back in a long plait, that hovered just above the ground. Her eyes were warm and brown, and Vinnie felt safe for the first time in weeks. She shuffled over to him and shot the Seeker a look of disappointment. Vinnie felt the relief of the heavy hands drop from his shoulders. She gently wrapped her tiny fingers around his hand and led him towards a large open door across the hallway.

"My name is Mrs Temple. Come with me my sweetheart, let me show you the garden." When they reached the open door, Vinnie was flooded with sunlight. As his eyes became accustomed to the brightness, he saw faces; a sea of faces all staring directly at him. Mrs Temple felt Vinnie's grip tighten.

"Don't be afraid my sweet, they are a friendly bunch." His grip loosened and Mrs Temple turned to give him a reassuring smile, but Vinnie Shadowsmith had vanished.

Vinnie wandered across the garden to an empty corner and sat on an upturned wooden box. He surveyed the garden with a saddened gaze. Life as he knew it had disappeared, and here he was, in a life chosen for him by someone else. His family were far away and lost to him. His home had become a flickering landscape in his mind. He feared time passing because he knew that image would fade. The thought of his mother and father's faces fading over time made his eyes fill with the salty tears he had promised not to cry. He shut his eyes and focused on what he remembered of them, revisiting every inch of their faces over and over again to make sure they were fixed in his memory for as long as possible.

He watched the children playing in the garden for hours, lost in his thoughts. He knew that they couldn't see him. He found solace in this. He also knew that they had seen him, and eventually he would have to show his face. But for now, he wanted to remain invisible, wanted to be alone until he knew who to trust. Until he had worked out how he was going to get out of here.

As his gaze swept across the garden, he noticed someone else sitting alone. In the corner directly opposite sat a tall girl with a steely stare. She seemed to be glaring directly at him. Her hair was long and thick with a fringe that flopped over her forehead. It was from beneath this fringe that her brilliant green eyes surfaced. Her skin was pale, the light seeming to dance across it, making her glow like a trapped firefly. But her lips pressed, cold and dormant. The dancing glow of her face seemed to skip her eyes and mouth. No upturned smile or longing sadness, she looked more lost than he did. Vinnie wondered how long she had been here. Not long he guessed, by seeing her demeanour. All the other children played in groups, but this girl sat alone. Every once in a while, he saw some of the other children whisper and glance up at her. Some giggled; some looked afraid, but none attempted to talk to her.

Gifted children usually arrived at the Academy on their sixth birthday, brought by parents who feared the gifts their children possessed, or by Seekers who swept the land looking for the gifted ones. But, like himself, this girl looked around 10 or 11 years old, and as if she had arrived quite recently. She didn't seem to know anyone, and he felt her silence speak to him. Vinnie's heart leapt as he realised that he may not be as alone as he thought. Maybe this girl had a soul as defiant as his. Maybe she had refused to come to Elmsmere as he had. With a skip in his step, he weaved his way across the garden and shuffled up next to her.

"I know you're there you know." Vinnie's head turned sharply. *How could she see him? He was invisible!* He didn't speak.

"You might as well answer me. I saw you sat over there all alone, swinging your legs in and out of the flower bed."

Vinnie snapped back with an accusing tone. "You didn't see me. That's cheating. You saw the plants moving where my feet were."

The girl laughed, "Well you're brighter than this bunch of idiots then. They didn't even notice you'd disappeared. Look at them all rolling across the grass, playing tea with their dolls. You're in prison, you morons! And you're not getting out!" She kicked a stone at her feet and snarled.

"I'm Vinnie. Vinnie Shadowsmith," announced Vinnie, extending his hand and then quickly retracting it.

"Look Vinnie, I know you looked over here and thought, *ooh she's alone like me, maybe she wants to be friends*. Well I don't."

Vinnie had never been one to shy away from a challenge. He loved a challenge, and he particularly liked this one. "You are making a lot of assumptions there. It's a bit presumptuous of you to assume I want to be your friend. I might have just been coming over to ask you what time dinner is. I could hardly ask one of this lot, could I? Why don't we start with your name?"

She turned to him, brushing her heavy fringe away from her eyes. "Kitty. It's Kitty Midnight." Kitty jumped up to her feet, brushed the back of her trousers, and walked away. "Oh and Vinnie… Dinner's at six."

Vinnie had been invisible for four days and spent most of that time plotting his escape. He had mapped out every door and every window, listed every lock on every gate, and had memorised the daily rota of every staff member.

At night he would lie on his bunk and watch out of the small window across from him. The ten-foot-high brick wall surrounding the Academy blocked a large part of his view, but, just over the brim of it, he could see dark woodland, and his way home.

Kitty either ignored him or was behaving as if he wasn't there, which was fine by him. He was going to escape with or without her. She was the one missing out not him. If she wanted to stay locked in this prison, so be it. He was starting to think he was wrong about her anyway.

On the fifth day of his stay at Elmsmere, he lay silent in his bunk waiting for the others to head for breakfast. He watched, as, one by one, the children awoke, rummaged in the numbered boxes under their bunks for clothes, socks, and shoes, and then dressed themselves. The boys licked their hands and smoothed down their hair, while the girls ran fingers through theirs and scooped it up into a varying assortment of plaits, ponytails, and bunches. They scuttled out of the room one by one, tumbling hungrily along the hallway and down the stairs towards the dining hall.

When everyone was gone, he leapt from the bunk and raced towards the nearest set of beds. Rummaging frantically in the boxes, his fingers felt for straps or buckles. Eventually, he dragged out a small satchel. The size was not ideal, but he didn't have time to be fussy.

Suddenly he heard footsteps tramping towards the door. He grabbed the bag and stuffed it under the nearest bed, scrabbling in after it. He lay quietly, stifling his breathing and slowing his heartbeat as he had done so many times before.

"He must be in here the little freak. Hello little vanishing boy, where are you?" The room erupted in laughter.

"I'm serious!" the first voice demanded, "We could use that invisible kid; he'd fit right in with us."

A second voice spoke, his voice faltering, "Chordata, how are we going to find him if we can't see him?"

Chordata paused. There was a loud thump and a whimper, "Sorry Chordata."

Chordata paced slowly around the room. Vinnie knew she was searching for signs of his presence: a wafting curtain, a creased pillow, an indented mattress. When she found nothing, she ordered the others to leave. "He's not here, stupid kid. He's probably stealing his breakfast from the kitchen. Why he won't just eat with us I have no idea."

Once the door had closed, Vinnie crawled out from under the bunk clutching his satchel. He had seen Chordata in the garden over the last few days, and watched her little underlings follow her around aimlessly, executing her every instruction. He would never follow anyone like Chordata Weavil.

Two days earlier, Vinnie had been sat on his box in the garden, sharpening a stick ready for his trip, when he noticed one of Chordata's cronies slithering up to two of the younger children at the Academy. They sat on a small patch of grass away from everyone else looking lonely and afraid. They were seeking comfort in plaiting each other's hair. The smallest one had a comb that she had concealed in her pocket. She stroked it gently, as if somehow it would console her in the loss of her family. She passed it slowly through her new friend's hair, untangling all the tiny knots gently, leaving it smooth and soft.

Chordata's henchman came up behind the young girl. He wrenched the comb from her hand.

"Sorry, but all property round here is owned and loaned by Chordata Weavil." He gestured towards the doorway where Chordata leaned. Her red hair flickered in the breeze, setting the sky alight as the sun caught it. Her sharp nose and jagged chin seemed to point accusingly wherever she looked. She opened her eyes wide, and waved, giving a wry smile.

"You wanna borrow anything from Chordata, including this 'ere comb, then you just pop over later. 'Course, there's a fee, mind," smirked the henchman.

The girls winced as he stepped towards them. "Chordata looks after her own you know girls and you'd do well to be part of that."

He scuffed the grass with his feet as he walked away, kicking dust and mud into the air. The girls sat rigid as the filth rained over them.

Vinnie watched and felt the gut-wrenching guilt associated with doing nothing, but he couldn't risk being seen before his escape. He needed to keep a low profile.

Vinnie started filling the satchel with the food he had been smuggling from the kitchen over the last few days. He added his sharpened sticks, a bottle of water, and a jumper. He rolled out a rope he had made from rolled-up sheets from under his bunk. At one end, he had weighted it with some books from the library and as he hurled it out of the window as hard as he could, he heard the satisfying thud of the book bundle thumping into the bricks, hooking around the iron rail on top of the wall. He tugged at the rope ready to begin his departure.

As he prepared to leave, he dropped his satchel and slipped across the room to its darkest corner, where Chordata's bunk sat. Nestled between boxes and trunks filled with trinkets she had pilfered from others; her bed was piled with warm blankets and soft furs. He sneered as he noted the other beds, bare in comparison, each with a plain sheet and rough blanket. He shook his head to shuffle away the thoughts of injustice. Concentrate Vinnie, concentrate. He fumbled around in a box under the bunk, until he felt what he was looking for. He glided back to the window, passing two small, neat beds lined up against the wall. As he passed, he dropped a small comb into a box under the beds. He grabbed the satchel, slid down the rope, and disappeared over the wall.

Chapter 2: Who is Vinnie Shadowsmith?

Vinnie landed with a thump, scraping his arm down the wall as he dropped. He felt the warm, wet dribble of blood as he clambered to his feet. The bright sunlight of the morning seemed to have been absorbed by the dark, woody canopy of the forest and Vinnie was plunged into darkness. The trickle of blood snapped him into consciousness. He felt around for the makeshift rope. He tore a strip of the sheet away, quickly wrapping and tying it around his wounded arm, inhaling sharply as it tightened.

He moved slowly along the wall, his eyes gradually becoming more accustomed to the darkness. Getting away from Elmsmere was his priority, but his heart was beating so quickly that his arm was throbbing with every pulse. As he came to a stop, he leaned against the wall breathing deeply. He reached down to his wrist and felt for his periapt. The soft leather felt warm between his fingers. As he ran his fingertips across the smooth crystal, he closed his eyes.

....

17

Vinnie's father had been blessed with The Sense. As a baby, he would smile as gifted children walked by, and outstretch his arm in an attempt to brush their skin. He felt it as a warm glow that passed over him like a sun-blushed wind. As he aged, the sensations he felt remained the same but his abilities to interpret them strengthened. Alongside the warm glow came a vision that allowed him to see the gift and its abilities, knowing by the touch of their skin whether the gift drew its strength from the darkness or the light.

On his thirteenth birthday, he was told by his father that he needed to make a choice: that The Sense was special. Those who were blessed with it must choose a life path, that would ensure it was not wasted. Vinnie's father had always known this day would come and he knew inherently which path he would choose. He had seen the Seekers visit the village every year for as long as he could remember. He had felt the tension and sadness fill the air in the days leading up to their arrival. Mothers would hide in corners, weeping into their hands at the impending loss of their children. Fathers would stoop slowly about their business, grumbling gently as they passed friends and family, preparing for the loss to come.

The Seekers would slink into the village at the dead of night, shuffling around the dwellings, breathing deeply to identify the gifted children within. The following morning, they would knock twice on the doors of the gifted ones, and, placing a firm hand on the shoulder of the child, they would lead them away from the village, to the harrowing wails of the mourning mothers and fathers. Vinnie's father could never cause that amount of pain to any family. So he chose the alternate path, the life of a periapt maker.

Every village had a periapt maker. It was their job to determine if a child was born with a gift. Within the first week of a child's birth, their parents would bring them to a periapt maker to discover their fate. The periapt maker would then style a periapt for the child to be worn as a reminder of home, and a link to the family that loved them. Although a bearer of bad news, Vinnie's father always ensured that the periapts he made were as beautiful as the children who wore them. He always felt that if there was only one thing he could do for these lost souls, then he would ensure that he did it right.

Vinnie's father knew that his wife was pregnant before she did. He hid his sadness with a forged smile when she told him. He gathered her up into his arms and buried his head into her soft hair.

He studied every inch of her blissful gaze, as she gently caressed her stomach over the passing months, and locked that image within his memory. He knew that there was every chance he would never see it again.

On the day of Vinnie's birth, his father gently stroked his son's face, and winced as he felt the warm glow melt across his body. He glanced at his wife, and, with that one look, she knew. Her eyes dropped to the ground, and she wept silently as not to wake her new son.

For three days she refused to hold him for fear of forging a bond, and his father was forced to feed him on goat's milk. Vinnie's father could not bear to see his wife in such pain so he decided that he would hide his son from the Seekers. His wife was unsupportive at first, not believing that anyone could fool the Seekers. But his father's plan was the only plan they had, and, considering his knowledge and abilities, his wife relied on hope and belief that it would work. Vinnie's gift would certainly help, and what choice did they have?

His parents told neighbours and family that their child had died at birth. Vinnie's mother's genuine tears of grief supported their tale, quelling the suspicions of those around them. Vinnie was a quiet child; no, Vinnie was a silent child. It was as if he had an innate understanding of the danger of his cries and so he communicated to his mother with looks, smiles, and silent tears.

As he grew, he matured into his gift, and, when able to control it fully, he was able to walk amongst the villagers. He loved to listen to their ambling conversations in the square, discussions about everything and nothing, gossip about the neighbours and their hopes and dreams for the future. He would sit for hours soaking up the warm sunshine and even warmer conversation.

Every year when the Seeker's visit was due, his parents would walk him into the forest where he would climb to the top of an old oak tree and hide within a hollowed-out knot.

At first, he was afraid of the forest with its dark and daunting silence. But his father held him close and whispered in his ear. "Remember Vinnie, never be afraid of what you cannot see. Darkness is a friend that will shroud you from harm and the forest is a brother who will guide you home."

As his sixth birthday came and went, Vinnie spent more time wandering through the village, his parents becoming confident that it was possible to keep his secret forever. The villagers became his unknowing friends. He was close to them in their happiest moments and their deepest sorrow. He shared birthdays, celebrated weddings, and, although he could not speak to them, he never felt alone.

One dark morning, Vinnie's mother rang the bell that called Vinnie to breakfast. Getting no response, she rang again and waited for him to meander down the stairs and take his seat at the table. When he didn't appear, she became anxious and clambered the stairs to his room. What if they had taken him? The door flew open as she rushed into his room. His bed was sodden with sweat. He lay huddled in a bundle, shivering with fever. Liquid trickled down the side of his face and across her fingers as she stroked his cheek. Hours passed and his condition worsened, his skin becoming pale and cold as he slipped into unconsciousness. By the time his father had returned from work, his mother was desperate and hysterical. She felt they had no choice but to take him to the doctor. She could not let him die.

The doctor prescribed a tonic to bring down the temperature, and some treatments to apply to his now fragile skin. He was sworn to secrecy, and, having lost a child of his own to the Seekers, he empathised with their plight. His wife however was not so understanding. Riddled with jealousy she sent word to the Seekers.

That night, without warning, the Seekers scuttled into the village and posted themselves outside the door of the periapt maker. The following morning the family awoke to the foreboding double knock they had hoped never to hear.

Vinnie was the first to hear it. In that slumber between sleep and awareness, he heard the double knock. Unaware and unafraid, he stretched his legs as far as he could, feeling the damp icy air on his toes. He snapped them back under the blankets and shivered through a satisfied yawn.

It was then he heard his mother's footsteps chatter across the hallway as she mumbled, "No… No… No… No… Not now." And he knew. His grin dropped, and he fumbled out of bed, landing with a thump.

He gasped for breath as he heard his father shouting, "LEAVE. I SAID LEAVE! You are mistaken."

He cowered as he felt the crash of his father being slammed against the wood of the front door. His head dropped when the hinges creaked as the old door fought back. A low howl began to form, starting as a whimper, and cascading into an unbroken squeal; his mother unable to conceal her pain.

The Seekers found him cowered in the corner of his room, too afraid to vanish and damp with his silent tears. He was as quiet as he had always been, but this time there was no hiding. A Seeker knows. You cannot hide.

His mother shrieked as she clung to the Seeker's legs and begged them not to take him. But the gathering villagers knew it would change nothing, as did Vinnie's father. He gently unclasped his wife's fingers from the Seeker's ankle. He sat her on the ground where she wept uncontrollably into her hands. He took Vinnie by the wrists and clasped him close to his chest.

He whispered softly into his ear. "Be brave my son, as you always have been. Remember, never be afraid of what you cannot see. Darkness is a friend that will shroud you from harm and the forest is a brother who will guide you home."

He slipped a periapt over Vinnie's hand, and tightened the leather around his wrist. Vinnie looked down to see the smooth crystal glint, as the early morning light reflected from the sharp curves of the eagle's talons.

"I know you will fly home to me one day, my son." his father shouted as the Seekers led Vinnie away.

....

25

Vinnie's pulse had slowed, and his mind had sharpened. He opened his eyes and gripped the periapt tightly. "I'm coming home," he mumbled as he strode forwards into the darkness.

The forest air felt damp on Vinnie's warm skin and his neck began to sweat, sending rivulets of water trickling down his back. He twitched with irritation as he stumbled through the forest, parting the canopy in his path.

The darkness began to open up, and a soft light became visible in the distance. Drawn to it like a bumbling insect he increased his pace. The closer it got, the faster he moved. The ground began to level out and the surrounding bushes became smaller and sparser.

The source of the light was an opening between two large trees, whose leafless branches twisted together to form a tall archway leading to a large clearing. The thick trunks framed a view so incredibly beautiful that Vinnie stepped back to take it all in. He took a deep breath before moving forward.

Beneath his feet lay a sea of flowers that carpeted the ground like a delicate rainbow. Large blue petals with thin green stems, tiny red blossoms with large dark hearts, and oval yellow buds on the cusp of bloom swam amongst rivers of green leaves. He ran his fingers across the delicate petals and felt a calmness he hadn't experienced before. He closed his eyes and let the sensation sweep over him, enjoying his first ever moment of peace. He began to move slowly across the clearing, the flora gently caressing his ankles as he passed.

The flowers began to move rhythmically against his legs as he walked, their stems lengthening until they began brushing against his calves. The yellow buds began to climb out from the lawn, and, in spectacular unison, their flowers opened revealing a bright orange core. Their vine-like stems began wrapping themselves around Vinnie's legs, reaching up towards his arms. Tiny red petals began toying with his fingertips, creeping across his hand and around his wrists. Vinnie began to feel anxious, but his body seemed powerless, lethargic and weary. The vines started to tighten, drawing him towards the ground. Unable to fight them, Vinnie slumped as the flowers strengthened their grip, pulling him flat to the damp earth below. Creepers shot out from underneath him, sweeping around his chest, pinning him down. Within seconds his body became swamped with bright petals and blooms.

Suddenly the feeling of calm vanished and Vinnie felt a rush of panic. He began struggling against the thick stems entwined around his arms, but he was unable to shift them. A long thin vine began to tighten around his neck and the panic became breathless hysteria. He closed his eyes and pictured his mother chuckling as she danced around the kitchen with his father. He smiled as he gasped for his last breaths.

Chapter 3: A Viney Rescue

The strange clicking noise he heard seemed distant and inhuman. It became frantic, and its pitch and volume increased until it reached a screech of clicks, interspersed with a buzzing hum. Its intensity vibrated through Vinnie's body, jolting him into consciousness. He began to struggle, to no avail, and the feeling of helplessness returned. He opened his eyes, and through a screen of petals, he could see a shadow moving above him; waving around wildly. This dark shadow seemed to be the source of the horrific squeal. Vinnie began to feel even more afraid.

All of a sudden, the vines loosened their grip, slithering back into the undergrowth. He felt them slide across his body as they unravelled their tendrils from his fingertips, and slowly released him from their grip. He reluctantly opened his eyes, blinded by the bright sunlight that was streaming around the shoulders of the dark figure looming above him.

"It's ok, Vinnie, take your time." Unexpectedly, the voice was soft and warm. "Slowly sit up and take my hand. It's ok."

29

Vinnie rose sluggishly and reached out to grasp the stranger's hand. The hand was small, and as he glanced upwards, he recognised a girl from the garden at Elmsmere. She was slender and delicate, reminding him of the vines that had held him to the ground. Her long blonde hair was tied back with tiny flowers that seemed to move slowly through it, entwining themselves into the golden strands. Her skin was fair and her eyes an icy blue. She was magnificent.

She smiled kindly, "I'm Lilana, are you feeling ok?"

Vinnie glanced into the field which had returned to its original intoxicating state of beauty after the horror. Fear pulsed through his body, and he stumbled backwards, tripping awkwardly over his feet, until he finally settled upon an upturned log. Lilana floated alongside him, holding him gently; she sat beside him and placed his satchel by his feet.

"I'm sure they wouldn't have killed you; just stopped you in your tracks so to speak. They are… the plants are … well, gentle creatures incapable of real harm. I can't be certain of course, but I'm pretty sure."

Vinnie took a deep breath, closed his eyes, and exhaled slowly and deliberately.

"It's their job you see, to protect us. They need to keep us safe. Keep us… well… safe… safe here."

Vinnie snapped into consciousness, "This is keeping me safe?! How is strangling me to death keeping me safe?! " His voice echoed through the trees. "We need to move. Do that clicky, shrieky thing again and get us out of here. I need to get back to my father." He scooped up his satchel and slung it over his shoulder, as he grabbed Lilana's wrist. "Let's go."

Lilana remained rooted to the ground, her arms swaying as Vinnie tugged at her wrist.

"What is wrong with you? Seriously!" Vinnie complained as he let her wrist drop to her side. "We have to get moving before they realise we are missing. I cannot sit there and do nothing for one more day, I don't belong here."

Lilana swept loose wisps of hair away from across her face as Vinnie gave her a desperate

31

look. "I know you want to see your family, but I can't leave here Vinnie," Lilana shifted uneasily. "I am safe here at Elmsmere. It is my home and I have nowhere else to go."

"What about your family? How can you have just forgotten them so quickly?! Surely they are your home?" Vinnie questioned.

Lilana smoothed her skirt and looked up at the impatient face beside her. "I am not like you, Vinnie. Seekers did not knock on my door and drag me from my family. My family brought me here themselves. They were afraid of my gift, embarrassed even. They thought me strange, and difficult, and they certainly did not love me. I have never known the love of family, well, not really," she muttered towards the ground. "But I know the closest thing I have are the four walls of Elmsmere and the people within it. I am quite normal here and I belong. Vinnie, I cannot leave with you. You must venture on alone… but If the plants and trees don't get you, the terrible Clodwalkers will."

She placed her hand on the red sodden cloth surrounding his arm. "Come back with me, at least for now, so we can get your arm seen to.

Maybe you can find someone else to help you on your return?"

Vinnie stood defiant as he grabbed his satchel, wincing in pain as his arm struggled to take the load. "I can't go back, I just can't. I cannot sit for another day watching child after child blunder about as if they deserve this. It's a prison, Lilana, don't you get that?"

"It is your prison, Vinnie, but it is my home. Just as you did not want to leave yours, I do not want to leave mine. I am not the right person to take you on this journey. I'm sorry."

"And where exactly am I going to find another person who can talk to trees, heh? Is there someone else at Elmsmere? Or do I just wait until someone else turns up with weird plants wiggling through their hair?!" As soon as he had said it he regretted it. He spat it out before he could think. This hurtful sentence, born of his own fears, could not be taken back. The silence pulled at his conscience.

"Vinnie, I am not the right person," whispered Lilana as she began walking back towards the Academy.

33

Vinnie felt defeated, but he knew that he couldn't journey on alone. He had limited knowledge of the forest, and Clodwalkers, whatever they were, sounded less than friendly. He closed his eyes and thought of his father, willing himself not to give up, and reminding himself that there would be another way.

"I'm sorry," he muttered as he grabbed her hand.

Vinnie and Lilana ambled back silently along the wall in the darkness. Lilana held his hand in hers as he followed the path that she showed him. Eventually, they arrived at a wooden gate that creaked open on their arrival. As they passed through, it seemed to sigh with relief, which led Vinnie to turn his head back as it closed. Vines slithered up from the ground and wound their way across the gate, sealing it shut behind them. Lilana slipped a key into her pocket, as Vinnie looked away. He turned ahead to see the red brick of Elmsmere, as sadness and disappointment set in once more.

He heard the rustle of Mrs Temple's enormous overskirt as she grabbed his arm from behind. "Oh my goodness sweetheart, what has happened here?" Vinnie still unable to speak for fear of crying just looked down at his arm.

"He fell in the garden, Mrs Temple. He was helping me tend to the vegetable patch when he tripped against the wall. He is a little shaken up."

Mrs Temple smiled knowingly as if she had seen it many times before. "Oh, poor lamb. You come with me and I'll dress it properly. Come, come."

As Vinnie was led away, he glanced at Lilana. She smiled gently and waved her fingers by her side as a half-hearted farewell. *'I deserved that,'* he thought.

Chapter 4: The Escape Plan

Kitty felt sad when she saw him. He looked crushed, the hopeful spring in his step replaced with the same dragging tread as the rest of them, lumbering day to day, wondering where their families were, and what they were doing. Watching him resigning himself to a life at Elmsmere was hard to watch. Kitty felt uncomfortable. Normally she didn't care, or rather she forced herself not to care.

But Vinnie was different, and she felt it. He wasn't willing to move to the same beat as the rest of them, accepting their fate, and pretending that their worlds hadn't come crashing down. He could see beyond the wall. Like her he had attempted to scale it. But like her, he had failed to get far. As she watched him drift into the dining room and drop down into his seat, she realised that she felt uncomfortable because, in essence, she was watching her own demise. She too had given up. Watching him slog his way through existence was like looking in a mirror.

"Morning, Houdini," chuckled Chordata as she shoved her way onto the seat next to Vinnie,

36

closely followed by two spindly critters that sniggered as she spoke. "I hear you fell off a wall like Humpty Dumpty." More sniggers erupted from Chordata's cronies as Chordata tried to catch Vinnie's eye. Vinnie slowly ate his porridge, not bothering to glance up. "Then got pinned down by some pansies," she laughed. Vinnie continued taking mouthfuls of sweet porridge, refusing to be drawn in. That is exactly what she wanted. "If your Daddy could see you now, eh Vinnie. He's probably glad that a pathetic excuse for a son like you was brought here. Saves him a job."

Vinnie leapt up, his chair crashing against the wall behind him as he lurched towards Chordata. Kitty grabbed his shoulder, pulling him back.

"Do we need to talk about your failed escape, Chordata?" she asked as Chordata's smile briskly vanished. "Didn't it involve a puddle and a duck?" Stifled giggles rippled around the room.

"I was seven!" slammed Chordata as she scraped her chair across the floor. "And I was still braver than this joke." She grabbed a bread roll from the table and strolled away. "Come on you lot.

These pathetic excuses for gifted kids are boring me even more than usual," she snapped as she strolled away.

Kitty rolled her eyes and smirked as she watched Chordata leaving, shoving her underlings forward while scolding them. "Morning Vinnie," she murmured as she sat down. He turned to face her. She noticed that the table was silent and all eyes were fixed on them. She scowled at them. "What!" Everyone snapped back to their conversation as quickly as they had stopped.

"Err, morning," he replied. "To what do I owe this pleasure? Come to gloat about my failed escape too? Go ahead and tell me what an idiot I am and how pointless it all is. I'm all ears."

"Giving up so easily are you?" she whispered as she took a mouthful of porridge.

He wiped his mouth as the anger rumbled up from his gut for the second time this morning, filling his chest with a tightening rage. "And what would you know?!" he snapped quietly. "From what I've heard, you are no different. One failed attempt and you sit in the corner sulking. You are no different to me, Kitty Midnight."

Kitty leaned in closely. "Well, I certainly am no different, Vinnie," she retorted "And maybe that's the point."

Surprised, Vinnie stared at Kitty as she paused. For the first time since they had met, Kitty's eyes were alive. She gave him a small but definite smile. "Tonight," she whispered. "Six o'clock in the library."

Kitty felt alive for the first time in months. She had hope, and that little bit of herself that she had lost came creeping back.

He arrived promptly, looking eager to discuss their potential escape. She spotted him in the arched doorway, framed by the wooden dragon spiralling its way around the doorframe. He looked small and insignificant, but his eyes were full of strength and determination. She knew that this was her chance. She beckoned him over to the table where she sat, surrounded with dusty old books left open on yellowing, curled pages.

"Is it safe to talk here?" he whispered, "It seems very open."

Kitty giggled, "No one comes in here. In fact, the only person I've seen in here in eight years is you collecting books to throw over the wall."

Vinnie's face glazed a little crimson, and then he gasped, "Eight years! You've been here for eight years?!"

Kitty smiled, "Actually I've been here for 11 years, dropped off as a baby on the steps."

"I'm so sorry," Vinnie sighed, "That's awful."

"Well, I had 11 years to hatch my escape plan, and it still failed," Kitty laughed. "That should make you feel better about yours."

They both leaned back in their seats and chuckled. Kitty felt a warmth she had never experienced. The warmth of friendship.

"How did you get caught?" Vinnie asked, "Was it that awful field of flowers? Lilana saved me you know."

"I know," she nodded. "Our stories are similar, but it was Lilana's sister Iris that saved me."

"Lilana has a sister? I haven't seen her." Vinnie looked confused, "I thought she had no family?"

"She's gone, just like they all do eventually. No one knows where or why, and I have no intention of being next." Kitty was more focused now.

"What do you mean gone?" asked a confused Vinnie. "People don't just disappear!"

"Haven't you noticed that everyone here is young? That there is no one over 12 years old."

Vinnie thought back to breakfast; tables filled with young children gobbling down porridge. She was right. The faces he saw slurping on their goblets of milk were much younger than Kitty and himself. How had he not noticed?

When you hit 12 years old, then it's time. For what, I don't know. But the Seekers return and they take you. Vinnie, we have a month to get out of here before I am taken. Will you help me?"

Vinnie gave an excited smile. "As if you even needed to ask."

Kitty smiled back. She felt hopeful but knew that, however detailed and clever a plan she and Vinnie concocted, there was one big sticking point. The meadow of flowers surrounded the entire building, and they would be drawn in and

41

smothered before they made it across the field. The only hope they had was Lilana.

Kitty had been lucky before and she knew it. Iris had the sight, a rare gift that enabled her to see for miles. She would watch out across the fields and into the woods, gazing at and beyond the horizon for hours. She had been watching from her window when she had spotted Kitty, hobbling through the woods towards the meadow, dragging her leg behind her. She had seen many escape attempts. She knew how they ended. Even without the injured leg, Kitty had no chance against the meadow of vines.

Knowing the danger Kitty was in, Iris crashed through the forest after her, galloping through the trees like a wild pony. She spotted Kitty staring longingly at the alluring carpet of petals in front of her, and coming up behind Kitty and grabbing her waist, she dragged her backwards, knocking her to the ground.

Kitty lay face down in the dirt, gasping for air like a grounded fish. Her knee cried scarlet tears from a deep gash suffered during her drop from the wall. The blood was cascading down her shin forming a small pool at her feet. Her head flopped forward in defeat as she knew that she could go no further.

She mumbled, "Take me back. It's ok." Iris pulled her arm up over her shoulder and dragged her back through the woods and through the gate of Elmsmere.

Her thoughts returning to the present, Kitty knew there was only one way. "We need to get Lilana to come with us. It's the only way we can get through the meadow. There is no one else here with a gift that can get us through."

Vinnie huffed, "Lilana and I are not exactly friends. She doesn't want to escape; she wants to stay here." He shot a shameful glance towards the door. "I said some things I shouldn't have."

Kitty placed a reassuring hand on his shoulder, "Look we can undo the things we say in the heat of the moment when we don't mean them. She saved your life, and you will always owe her that. You need to start with an apology."

Vinnie shifted in his seat, "What about your gift? Can't we use that?"

Kitty's smile dropped. Her eyes fell to the table and her fringe swept over them, hiding her again from Vinnie's prying eyes. "I don't know what it is," she muttered. "I was dropped here at midnight wrapped in a blanket with this." She pulled up her sleeve to reveal a bright green crystal periapt. It was a small cat with black eyes, poised to pounce. It was held on a gold cord, twinkling as the light flickered.

"Wow!" Vinnie exclaimed. "That is something else." His father had made some beautiful periapts, including one for the chief of the village's daughter out of black crystal, that hung on a silver chain. But this green crystal was quite something to behold.

"Yes well, it seems I have an amazing periapt and a mediocre gift," mumbled Kitty. "So mediocre in fact that it hasn't bothered to appear." She looked up expectantly to see Vinnie's pitiful gaze, but instead, he looked excited.

"I cannot wait to see what it's going to be," he grinned. "This is going to be one hell of an adventure!"

Lilana had seen them watching her over breakfast, glancing up from their plates and smiling. She was pleased to see them happy and positive, after they had both tried so hard to leave and failed. It was good to see them finally accepting what they had, and even embracing it. Vinnie hadn't eaten properly for days, nibbling at the odd crust of bread aggressively. To watch his suffering had made her want to hug him and let him know that it would be ok. She had even considered dropping some of her Nora flower juice into his water to give him a lift, but she knew it would only last a few hours and he needed to accept his fate to be truly happy.

His face now radiated hope, and Kitty too looked less jaded than before. Who knew a kinship could bring such joy to two people?

She collected her bowl and glass and carried them over to the counter. "Thank you," she smiled "It was delicious as always."

Mrs Temple grinned. "Always so polite, Lilana," she smiled.

Chapter 5: Lilana's Revelation

Lilana glided away and out into the garden. Her smile was unflagging, and as she swept her skirt under her legs, she drifted down onto the grass, wriggling her toes amongst the dull green blades. She swept her hands through the flower bed, sighing as she felt the leaves and petals tickle her fingertips.

"Nice Noras." Lilana startled and opened her eyes. The plants shrunk back from her hands.

"Pardon?" she asked.

"I like your Nora flowers," muttered a nervous Vinnie.

Lilana turned to face him. "Thank you," she smiled. "It's nice to see you feeling more yourself."

Her warmth towards him rinsed his guilt with a shower of shame that he couldn't shake. "I'm so sorry," he apologised, meaning it more than ever. "I shouldn't have said what I said and upset you. It wasn't right and I'm really sorry."

Her lips curled upwards in forgiveness. "It's ok, Vinnie, we always lash out when we are afraid." He felt relieved by her kindness and understanding. "I'm just glad that you have moved on and understand that Elmsmere is your home," she beamed.

Vinnie paused, blinked, and swallowed, not quite believing what he was hearing. "Elmsmere is not my home, Lilana, and neither is it yours." Lilana's smile dipped a little in disappointment. "Lilana, you have to see that this place is keeping you away from the world, hiding you from who you should be with."

Lilana stood up and dusted off her skirt. "Have you ever considered that maybe I want to hide?"

Vinnie gulped as he watched the vines in Lilana's hair begin to twist erratically, pulling away from her face as she spoke. "I don't want to live in a world where people look strangely at me. I don't want to be the odd one, the one that no one speaks to. My parents left me here because they were afraid of me, just like you are now."

Vinnie realised that he had gone too far and said too much. He started to creep backwards. Lilana shook her head and whispered undetectable words to herself over and over. She looked at the door and ran towards it.

Realising he was losing her, Vinnie panicked. "What about Iris?" he shouted. "Don't you want to see her again? You can come with us."

Lilana spun around, her hair leading the way, "Vinnie, she left me too, she left me too." She sobbed as she ran into the empty dining hall and up the stairs, the door slamming shut behind her with a thud.

Lying on her bed, Lilana wept into her pillow, attempting to stifle her sobs and sniffles. Why couldn't anyone see that she just wanted to be safe and away from prying eyes? That she wanted to be here with the other children and Mrs Temple. She had her garden and her flowers, and her freedom from judgement. She told Iris about that a hundred times and begged her not to run away, but she left anyway. Ran away and left her here alone.

She whimpered as she remembered snuggling up to her sister at night, safe in the warmth of her body heat. She longed to roll over and see her smiling back, but she knew she would never see her again. If she hadn't been suffocated by the vines, she would have been grabbed by the Clodwalkers. She could see what was out there, so

48

why did she take that risk? A soft wail leaked from Lilana's body, as she thrust her face deeper into the pillow.

When she awoke it was dark. It wasn't unusual for Lilana to sleep for long periods when she was upset, but all day seemed extreme even to her. Hungry and drowsy, she clambered out of her bunk, crept between the occupied beds surrounding her, and shuffled towards the kitchen. As she reached the top of the stairs, she stopped in her tracks to the sound of scrabbling and muffled squeals.

Leaning over the top of the bannister, she could see the bottom of Mrs Temple's plait swinging frantically. "Stop wriggling," she snapped, "You have no choice, It's time."

Chordata Weavil stood in the doorway, bag hoisted over her back, rolling her eyes and shaking her head. "For goodness sake, just knock her over the head or something, and let's get going."

Mrs Temple shot her a look. "Shhh." she whispered.

Chordata's eyes rolled again, this time accompanied by a loud tut. The frenzied scuffle

49

continued, and, in one last distraught attempt at freedom, an arm broke free of the struggle. As the arm forced its way towards the bottom step, making a desperate grappling motion, a large hand grabbed the wrist. Lilana immediately recognised the crimson velvet sleeve of a Seeker's uniform. She drew a sharp breath, silencing it with her hand pressed against her mouth.

The struggle it seemed was over. Mrs Temple picked up a small bag from the floor and handed it to the now silent child. Her face twisted with irritation, she instructed the Seeker to take the children outside.

As they opened the wooden door, the child turned to face Mrs Temple. "Why?" she pleaded. "Why me?"

Mrs Temple dusted down her white apron and looked her directly in the eyes. "It's not personal, Ella, it happens to you all. You are of age, and every gifted child takes the next path on their journey at 12. It's time to grow up."

Lilana stood startled, paralysed by what she had heard. Iris was 12. Iris was taken. Iris was alive. Her periapt caught the moonlight streaming up the stairs from the open doorway. The petals of the crystal flower danced across the ceiling, flickering from side to side as they caught Chordata's eye. She glanced upwards, and Lilana shuffled backwards into the shadows. Chordata smiled to herself as she turned and walked out into the night.

....

With the sweet smell of porridge filling her nose, Kitty spotted Vinnie from across the dining room and pulled up a seat beside him. "Well?" she asked, "How did it go?"

Vinnie winced. "Not exactly as we had hoped," he answered. "I think I caught her at the wrong time." He shuffled in his seat as he stirred his porridge. "Her mind seemed set, and I'm not sure we can change it."

Kitty spotted Lilana striding towards them. "I'm not sure what you said, Vinnie, but she looks a little bit irritated." As she approached, Vinnie cowered behind Kitty and peered over her shoulder.

Lilana stopped in front of them, smiled at Kitty and nodded at Vinnie. "I'm in," she announced. "When do we leave?"

<u>Chapter 6: And Then There Were Three</u>

Two children forming a friendship is passable, but three children constantly seen together is viewed more sceptically. Kitty had seen her fair share of escape attempts. Almost all of them had been foiled at the planning stage because of the suspicious behaviour of those involved. Kitty was determined that, having got beyond the wall once already, she was not going to be stopped before she made it there. So, when they met it had to be inconspicuous, seemingly unplanned, and quiet.

It was decided that Lilana was the most routine-led of the three. Any break from that routine would raise some questions. So the garden was the most obvious place to meet. Vinnie could remain completely inconspicuous, being invisible and all, so that just left Kitty.

It wasn't a secret that Kitty was less than sociable, until this time having no friends to speak of, and living a pretty isolated existence. It was decided that she would assume her normal position on a wooden box in the garden. However, she was not to speak. For Kitty even making eye contact

53

with Lilana would be beyond the realms of normal, let alone conversing. A plan was hatched where Kitty would use small physical gestures to indicate her thoughts. Over dinner Kitty and Vinnie allocated gestures to Kitty's thoughts; scuffing her feet against the mud suggested agreement, flipping her fringe meant disagreement, and standing up indicated she was absolutely, 100% opposed. Lilana spent most days talking to the plants, so having a conversation alone was no problem for her.

Lilana stood amongst a tall group of Elmberry plants, gently popping off the green fruit and slipping them into a drawstring bag. She felt the leaves rustle and knew he was there.

"Hi Vinnie," she chirped.

"Shhh!" he muttered, "Not so loud."

She smiled as the plants twittered. "No one can hear me, Vinnie, they don't even notice I'm here."

He relaxed a little as he glanced over to Kitty. "Can you hear us, Kitty?" he queried in a hushed whisper. The plants twittered again as

Kitty's feet scuffed across the mud in agreement. "Are they laughing at me?"

Lilana giggled and smiled. "They find your whispering a bit ridiculous to be honest. We are the only ones here." She gave the plants a dissatisfied glare and their leaves dropped to the ground. She stroked them in reassurance as they leaned against her.

"We need to make this short and sweet," mumbled Vinnie. "Our biggest issue is getting out. Since my leap of faith out of the bedroom window, they have been permanently shuttered and locked. Besides, both Kitty and I injured ourselves going out that way, and we need to be injury-free if we are going to make it."

As he paused for breath, Lilana leaned in. "I know a…"

"Yes, yes, I know it's a bit daunting, Lilana, but we all know the only way out is through the front." Lilana gasped as Kitty rapidly flipped her fringe.

"No, I don't think…" Lilana stuttered.

Vinnie put a firm hand on her shoulder. "It's the only way".

Kitty shot up and glared at the space where she assumed Vinnie would be, desperately trying not to shake her head.

Lilana sighed as Vinnie shook his head. "I have a key," she muttered.

"Pardon?" Vinnie dropped his arm. "To the front door, a key to the front door?" he asked.

"No," smiled Lilana as the plants twittered in chorus. "A key to the gate. Mrs Temple gave it to me so I could gather fruit, berries and firewood. She trusts me, you see."

Kitty sat down and rolled her eyes.

"That information could have been useful a few minutes ago," Vinnie tutted.

"Indeed," replied Lilana. "It would have been very useful, but unfortunately it was proving impossible to speak." Kitty scuffed her feet and smirked in agreement.

Vinnie shot Kitty a look. "So we have the way out. Now we need the when."

Lilana dropped down to pick some low growing fruit. "I think we need to leave it a while," she murmured. "It's only been a few weeks since your last attempt, and it's still very cold out there."

Kitty jumped to her feet again. Vinnie looked towards the stark, red brick of Elmsmere.

"Kitty hasn't got long, Lilana, they will be here to take her soon."

Lilana's shoulders slowly dropped, and the plants crept closer to hold her. "It's my home," her eyes drifted up to join Vinnie's. "And I'm afraid. I'm afraid I won't be able to save you from the meadow. I'm afraid the Clodwalkers will crush us. I'm afraid that I won't find Iris."

Kitty quickly glanced around and rushed to Lilana's side, grasping her hand tightly. "We will do this together," she whispered, "And we will find Iris."

"Tonight then," suggested Lilana feeling reassured. "Before I change my mind."

Lilana lay rigid, panting heavily into the dark. Desperately trying to slow her breathing so as not to draw attention to herself, she pinned the sheet tightly between her fingers. Inhaling more slowly, she focused her thoughts on the familiar, listing plants one by one in alphabetical order. This calmed her. She listened silently as the breathing of those around her become slow and heavy. She readied herself for the next move.

Shifting slowly to the edge of the bed, she lifted the blanket and slithered down to the floor, feeling around for her bag under the bed. She clasped the soft leather straps and dragged it gently out into the darkness of the room. She felt inside for the various pots of pollen, nectar, dried leaves, seeds and berries, feeling the comfort of knowing their power, and the sadness of leaving her garden behind. Closing the bag, she slipped it over her shoulder and crawled towards the doorway, weaving in and out of the small wooden beds.

Almost reaching the door, she sighed gently. As she reached up to the handle, a large bundle of blankets released a grunt that rumbled up the walls like a small earthquake, shifting blankets across the room as it disturbed those sleeping around her. She pulled the handle down and squeezed through the door so as not to drench the room in the light from the hallway.

The hallway was so quiet, that every step seemed to elicit a creak or groan that would be enough to wake the deepest of sleepers. She tiptoed lightly towards the stairs and trod gently onto the first step. The creak of the wood beneath her foot shuddered through her body, and she lifted it back quickly. Looking around her for another way, she anxiously glanced from corner to corner as her hand settled on the bannister. She rubbed it gently, smooth and shiny, and more importantly, quiet. She placed two hands on the handrail, shifted her bottom gently onto the bannister, and swept her hair away, across her shoulders. She looked up into the hallway nodding her goodbye as she shot down the bannister, making a gentle leap at the bottom. She bounded silently across the tiled floor towards the door to the garden. She turned the lock and snuck outside.

Vinnie saw her twitching nervously across the garden, glancing left and right as she scuffled towards the gate. As she approached the plants she tended daily, her walk changed. She drifted through the flowers as they brushed against her. He sensed sadness in her, loss almost. She reached the gate and smiled a greeting as Vinnie appeared before her. He touched her hand and she nodded in agreement to the unspoken pact between them.

Kitty strode across the garden, swinging a bag onto her shoulders. "Let's go," she whispered. Lilana plunged the key into the lock, the vines slithered away, and the gate swung open. They stepped out into the black, and, as they looked back for one final peek at Elmsmere, the gate slammed shut behind them.

Chapter 7: Who is Afraid of the Clodwalkers?

Lilana strode across the meadow, arms outstretched, murmuring and clicking rhythmically. The vines and flowers parted and entwined themselves with her fingertips as she passed, swaying gently to the tempo of her hypnotic melody. Vinnie and Kitty rushed nervously behind her huddled together, stumbling over each other's feet as they hurried to safety.

Beyond the meadow stretched a darkness, entangled with the knotty moss-stained branches of a thousand trees. The forest was damp and cold, the joyous celebration of the escape from the meadow short-lived, as the prospect of what lay before them quickly sunk in. Lilana pressed her hand on the scaly bark and paused, before her hand dropped heavily beside her.

"I can't feel them," she gasped. "They are dead: hollow, cold. It's sad."

"That explains a lot," Vinnie said as he slapped his hand against the nearest trunk. "No leaves, no blossom, no sound. What a weird place."

61

Lilana crouched to the ground and covered her face in a vague attempt to hide her fear. She rubbed her eyes and looked up at Kitty, who had been very quiet. She looked determined and ready, two things Lilana hadn't felt at all since this journey began. Kitty looked down and smiled.

"We can do this, Lilana. You've done your job protecting us, and now it's our turn to protect you." Kitty knelt down and held out her hand. As she helped Lilana to her feet she turned to Vinnie, "We need to be alert now, Vinnie. The Clodwalkers can be around any corner, and Lilana can't convince them not to hurt us. Our best option is to not let them find us."

Vinnie nodded in agreement. "No problem; quiet as a mouse me. Now let's do this!"

Kitty led the way, following what seemed to be some sort of overgrown pathway. They discussed whether taking the pathway was the best idea. But decided that at least that way they could see what was ahead of them, and behind them. The air was so moist that strands of hair kept sticking to their faces, lying flat and lank. The trees seemed to sweat, as streams of water trickled silently down their trunks to the damp earth.

They walked for hours and nothing changed. Wet faces, damp clothes, and a musty smell that caught in the throat. Vinnie started to cough, "Ahem… Ahem."

Kitty gave him a wide-eyed glare, putting her finger to her lips. "Shhh!"

"I can't help it!" he uttered as Kitty rolled her eyes. He swallowed several times but just couldn't shake the increasing choking sensation. He tried to clear his throat silently, but it just released a sort of muffled croak. Kitty shook her head as the croak became a low growl. A growl that got louder and louder.

She stopped, dropped her bag, and spun to face Vinnie. "Vinnie if you don't shut up you are going to attract the…"

Her sentence was finished with an ear-piercing scream from Lilana, who stumbled backwards and fell to the ground. Standing where Vinnie should be was a huge creature, whose head was lowered to the level of Kitty's shocked face.

Covered in dark, black fur, tipped with pale green moss, the creature blinked its one enormous, yellow eye and roared. The forest echoed and shook at the sound, and even the trees seemed to cower in terror.

Kitty turned to grab Lilana, as she saw her floating in the air, flying up the pathway. "Vinnie!" she shouted, "Head for the trees!" Lilana stopped mid-air, changed direction, and flew towards the trees as an invisible Vinnie thrust her in the direction of the undergrowth.

Kitty crashed through the woods towards Lilana, who she could see had leapt from Vinnie's arms now, and was racing through the undergrowth on her own steam. Behind they could hear the crushing of branches, as the Clodwalker thundered towards them.

"Keep running," Kitty cried. "Just don't stop!"

The stomps of the Clodwalkers increased and seemed to be coming from more than one direction, the echoes of the forest playing tricks, no doubt. Except each stomp sounded quite definite, and distinctive, and seemed to be closing in.

Lilana clambered through a small knot of branches, and tumbled into a large clearing, closely followed by Vinnie and Kitty. They sprinted towards the other side.

"Stop!" came a muffled voice from the side of the clearing. "Don't move. Stay exactly where you are."

Lilana skidded to an immediate halt. Vinnie and Kitty smashed into her. "What are you doing?" barked Kitty. "Are you crazy?!"

"Don't move and don't breathe," came the mysterious voice again.

"Don't breathe? What kind of ridiculous advice is that! How can they not breathe Mrs Muddles?" mumbled a different voice. "Good work, idiot. The Clodwalker won't kill them, but your ridiculous advice will."

The first voice tutted. "Shhh Gelda! You will put them off."

Vinnie turned towards the voices.

"I said don't move," squealed the first voice. "The Clodwalkers respond to sound and movement, but they cannot actually see much at all. Stay silent and still and we will help you."

Lilana gasped for breath and shuddered. She closed her eyes and held her breath, as Kitty squeezed her hand.

Two Clodwalkers scrabbled through the trees into the clearing, roaring to a halt as they threw confused looks around the opening. Kitty stared at their wrinkled faces, too frightened to look away. They had a permanent scowl, peppered with brown teeth that hung over their bottom lip like hungry stalactites. The yellow eye glinted between two long hairy ears, that hung down to their shoulders and swung as they moved.

From the side of the clearing appeared a small, flickering light. It danced across the clearing in a circle, twisting around and around the trapped children. The Clodwalkers spotted it and started striding towards the flashing spot. They began chasing it as it encircled the clearing, faster and faster, their circle widening towards the edge of the forest.

Kitty watched as they spun past her, stampeding across the earth and spitting dust across the clearing. The voices from the forest had silenced, and doubt began to nestle in her chest,

66

bringing with it anxiety and panic. Had listening to them been a big mistake? She noticed something edging its way into the clearing, creeping slowly out of the tree line towards the open ground. It was small and pink, difficult to make out. In its hand it held a long horn. It brought the horn to its lips and blew. A fine powder shot out as the Clodwalkers stormed by. The pink creature scuttled back into the woods.

The Clodwalkers marched on but their movement slowed. They seemed to stumble a little. Each step became more laboured and difficult. Their run soon became a slow walk. They dragged their feet through the dust and stretched their arms to the sky as they came to a halt, rubbing their eyes and scratching their ears. Then, out of nowhere, they flopped to the floor, rested their heads on each other's shoulders, and began to snore.

"Quickly, over here," shouted the pink creature. "Follow us." Kitty, Vinnie, and Lilana darted across the clearing as quietly as they could, following their rescuers into the darkness.

Gelda scampered across the forest bounding from trunk to trunk, grasping at branches to help her swing through the trees as quickly as possible. The ground was becoming greener now with bushes sprouting beneath her feet, and leaves rustling from the branches above. They were close. Mrs Muddles scuttled closely behind, keeping a sharp eye on the children that followed. When they reached the hollow, Gelda vaulted across the familiar mossy log and leapt up to grab a low hanging vine. As she grabbed the vine, it lowered, and the log lifted to reveal an empty hole.

Chapter 8: Down the Hole

"Jump in," she instructed. "Quickly now." Mrs Muddles stepped aside as Vinnie, Kitty and Lilana looked curiously into the hole. Lilana and Kitty looked reluctantly at each other, a look that Vinnie felt took too long and said too much. Without giving them another minute to decide he surged forward, arms outstretched, and shoved them into the hole, tumbling in behind them. Mrs Muddles jumped in to join them closely followed by Gelda as the log dropped down behind them.

"Woo hoo!" howled Vinnie as they slid down the tunnel into the darkness. He felt the soft ground graze his legs as they sped towards the pale glow beneath them. Kitty clasped her arms tightly around Lilana's waist as the air whistled past their cheeks, swirling their hair around their faces in gusts of exhilaration. Vinnie shut his eyes and let the wind blast away the panic and fear as he felt one step closer to seeing his family.

As the light came closer, they began to slow but it still felt like stopping was going to provide a bit of a challenge. Kitty dug her heels into the ground in front of her. "Dig your heels in," she

69

shouted as the earth began spitting soil and moss into the air. Vinnie plunged his heels down into the ground. They came grinding to a halt just as they hit the warming glow of the room below.

As Kitty clambered to her feet, she glanced around her. They were in a house of sorts with no windows or doors. It was like a hollowed-out burrow filled with furniture and knick-knacks and decorated with flowers, pots, pictures and small animals made of twigs.

Everywhere you looked was something that grabbed your attention. There was not one spot that didn't have an ornament or picture adorning it. It was like a warm and cosy museum. She smiled at this thought as she looked up at Vinnie and Lilana.

Vinnie was covered from head to toe in dark brown soil that sprinkled onto the floor as he moved. He was picking twigs from his hair and looking around aimlessly for a place to put them. Lilana's blond hair was now streaked with dark brown stripes and the vines that normally swayed and slithered through it were shaking in disbelief. Her face was green with moss. She had twigs stuck in the neck of her shirt like a collar of torture. They looked up at each other and, in that moment of realisation at how utterly ridiculous they looked, they erupted into laughter. They grinned as they began picking twigs from each other and disposing of them on a nearby table.

Gelda and Mrs Muddles bumbled into the hollow. Mrs Muddles clasped her hands together and grinned. "We finally have company," she smiled. "Get the kettle on Gelda."

Gelda was busy dropping a heavy curtain over the entrance to the tunnel. "I'll need to clear all these twigs off the table first," she grunted as she shuffled over to a small stove, sweeping the sticks into her arms as she passed. "Humph," she grumbled, as she filled a copper kettle and clunked it loudly onto a lit burner.

"We didn't mean to make a mess," apologised Lilana gently scooping up soil from the floor and looking quickly around for a bin. "You have a lovely home, you really do." Gelda gave another loud "Humph."

Mrs Muddles opened her arms and beckoned them over to a corner covered in blankets and cushions. "Sit, sit," she gestured. "You must be exhausted. Take a seat on the Slump." They willingly followed and plonked themselves down into the soft, pillow-like mound that swathed them in warmth. Gelda skirted towards them and shoved a cup of hot Elmberry tea into each of their hands.

As they sipped the hot, sweet liquid, they shuffled down further into the soft downy chair. Kitty looked at Lilana who had closed her eyes and sighed softly as she took another sip of the Elmberry tea. Gelda joined them and although still agitated seemed to settle a little as she drank.

"Shall we do some introductions?" asked Mrs Muddles immediately launching into her own. "I'm Mrs Muddles and this is Gelda. As I'm sure you know, we are Groggles. We live here in the hollow and…"

"Err, hang on," interrupted Vinnie "Scroll back a bit. I don't know if I'm just speaking for myself here, but I have no idea what a Groggle is." He looked towards Kitty and Lilana who were nodding their heads in agreement.

"Oh, I see," pondered Mrs Muddles looking a little confused. "Ok, well um, let's see."

"Humph, sounds about right," grumbled Gelda. "You people have wiped us from view so effectively that now we don't exist." She shook her head in disbelief and glugged down her tea in protest.

"Shhh, Gelda. It's not their fault, bless 'em." Mrs Muddles turned to the children. "Groggles are ground dwellers. We live in hollows underground and are peaceful folk. Unfortunately, as Gelda has badly explained…" She grimaced at Gelda. "Our digging skills and ability to spend large amounts of time underground has been noted by some of your folk. We are, in fact, some of the only Groggles left living free… Well, we think that is the case."

Kitty looked confused as she watched Gelda's wrinkled, pink skin turn a darkening shade of scarlet. Her large, round ears began to twitch and, as she shook her head, her grey curls flicked from shoulder to shoulder. Unable to contain herself she jumped to her feet. "Nope, nope, I'm not having it."

Stomping towards Kitty, she grabbed her wrist, tugging it sharply as she pulled up Kitty's sleeve. "This is the reason we are forced from our homes; stolen from our families and imprisoned underground in mines." She stared at Kitty's periapt as her rage turned to confusion.

"Where did you get this?" she accused. "Is it yours?" Mrs Muddles shuffled over lifting the periapt to get a closer look. "Who are you?" she asked taking two steps backwards. Gelda dropped Kitty's arm and joined Mrs Muddles.

Kitty quickly covered her periapt. "In all honesty, I don't know," she answered. "We have all escaped from Elmsmere Academy. Lilana was taken there by her parents; Vinnie was taken by the Seekers; and I was left there as a baby. Our story is not dissimilar to yours really. The Seekers come when we are 12 and take us away to who knows where, to do who knows what. We have escaped to find Vinnie's family and Lilana's sister."

Gelda looked uneasy. "And you? Where are you going? Who are your family?" she asked.

Kitty shrugged. "Like I said, I don't know."

Mrs Muddles held Kitty's hands and gave a gentle smile "It's ok to be lost," she replied reassuringly "It just means you haven't been found yet." Her warm, brown eyes soothed Kitty, but she still felt empty and alone. When Vinnie and Lilana found Iris and Vinnie's father what would that mean for her? She smiled an empty smile.

Gelda still looked unsure but had softened, "We will help you," she began "But if I were you, I would keep that periapt covered. It is very rare to come across a green crystal in the mines. It might draw the wrong attention. Regent Monelda would be very interested in someone with a green crystal periapt and you do not want her attention."

"Who?" Vinnie asked. "Who's she?"

Gelda rolled her eyes, exasperated by the apparent knowing of nothingness these children exhibited. "Regent Monelda? THE Regent Monelda? Your ruler and Queen?" She turned sharply to Mrs Muddles and shrugged in disbelief.

Mrs Muddles smiled calmly. "They are young and have a lot to learn that's all." She turned to Vinnie. "Monelda is the Regent. She runs the country and leads the people." Gelda scoffed.

75

Mrs Muddles continued. "It's a sad story really: her mother and father died when she was only 15. She had a twin sister, Emmeline, who passed shortly after, and, well, she didn't take it well."

Gelda shook her head back and forth huffing and puffing. "She is cruel, mean and vicious is what she is. Imprisoning our friends and family like slaves. We worked those mines for years with good wages, great food, and a place to sleep. We had homes and families; we were a community. She enslaved our people is what she did." Gelda stormed across the room, grumbling under her breath as she thundered through a curtain, leaving it to whirl about in the silence as she left.

Mrs Muddles spotted Lilana stretching her arms out and yawning silently. It was getting late, and the children looked exhausted. She began to pull out some of the pillows and plump them up by beating them against her legs. "I think it's time we got some sleep," she ordered. "It's been a busy day and we have a lot to plan tomorrow. You can sleep here on the Slump." She pointed to a curtained corner of the room that none of the children had noticed previously. "You can have a wash in there."

Lilana lay staring at the earthen ceiling thinking about Iris. All this talk of Regent Monelda and prison mines had awakened her worries. She felt her head swirl in anticipation of what would come next. Was this all a mistake? Could she return to the certainty of Elmsmere; to the comfort of Mrs Temple? No. No, it would be worth it when she found Iris. Kitty was kind and Vinnie was brave. The Groggles would help and she had her bag of course. She could do this. She pulled the blanket up to her shoulders and it stretched tightly across her toes as she drifted off to the muffled sounds of the gentle snores of the Groggles.

Chapter 9: Finding the Brotherhood

Gelda and Mrs Muddles let the children sleep while they prepared breakfast. Exhausted from the day before, the children snored and snuffled their way through the morning and finally awoke to the smell of freshly baked bread, and Mrs Muddle's special Muddled Eggs. They ate hungrily, stuffing chunks of bread greedily into their mouths, slurping the Muddled Eggs from the spoon.

"These eggs are amazing," spat Vinnie as he propelled wet crumbs across the table "What's in 'em?"

Mrs Muddles was thrilled. "Eggs, tree bark, dried moss, puddle water, and crushed dirt beetles," she beamed.

Vinnie stopped, mouth aghast, eggs dripping from his lips. Kitty kicked him under the table and he quickly wiped his chin. "Very filling them beetles, eh," he mumbled as he pushed his bowl aside.

"Delicious, thank you," praised Lilana as she guzzled down the last of her eggs giving a satisfied grunt. Vinnie looked at her astounded as she licked the bowl clean. Kitty gave him another sharp kick which made him leap up, banging his knee on the table as he rose.

"I'll clear up," he muttered as he tried to hold back the nauseating notion of beetles and muddy water for breakfast.

Once breakfast had ended, Gelda rummaged around in one of the many wooden cupboards, bringing out an old parchment that she untied and rolled out onto the table. "This is us here," she informed, pointing to the edge of the Dark Woods on the map. "Now do you have any idea where to find your father Vinnie, or your sister, Lilana?"

"All I know is that the Seekers took her," sighed Lilana. "Not much to go on I know."

"That's ok, dear," comforted Mrs Muddles. "It's a start. What about you, Vinnie, what was your village called?"

Vinnie thought to himself for a moment. That seemed like a perfectly reasonable question to ask, but actually, he had absolutely no idea. He had never in his time in the village heard anyone mention its name, and he had absolutely no idea

79

where it was. "Err, well. Well, it's called… Hmmm, now, let me think," he pondered.

"You don't know the name of it, do you?" Kitty shook her head. "You've been going on about going home all this time and you have no idea where home is! This is ridiculous."

Vinnie furrowed his brow. "I know where it is, I just can't remember. Hang on, it will come to me."

"He doesn't know!" Kitty shouted. "He doesn't know!" Lilana covered her ears and squeezed her eyes shut.

"Shhh," hushed Mrs Muddles. "That's quite enough." She gently stroked Lilana's hair. The vines wrapped themselves around her fingers. "What do you know, Vinnie?"

Vinnie slumped in his seat. Kitty's words ringing in his ears. He didn't know. "Ok, ok. I don't know where my village is, or its name, or anything about it. My father always said to me I could find my way home whenever I wanted to and I trusted that."

Kitty growled, "Great, well done. Great advice from your father there. Sounds to me like he doesn't want you to come home!"

Vinnie flew off his seat, lurching towards Kitty. "At least I have a home to go back to, Kitty Midnight!" he yelled. "What do you have? A glittery green crystal and a whole load of nothing!"

"Stop!" shrieked Lilana, tears welling in her eyes. "I thought we were friends and we had each other. We need to stick together and be the family we don't have right now. We can't fight, we just can't. We have nothing else but each other." She clasped Kitty's hand in hers and squeezed.

Vinnie dropped backwards into his seat. "The only thing my father ever said to me was 'Never be afraid of what you can't see. Darkness is a friend that will shroud you from harm. The forest is a brother who will lead you home'. I trust him."

Mrs Muddles leapt up. "Why didn't you just say that! You are from the Brotherhood."

"The what…?" asked Vinnie looking confused.

Gelda pointed to the dark woods on the map. "The Brotherhood live in a village inside the dark woods. It's their way of keeping people away. It's said that only members can find their way there. Oh, and those grim Seekers of course. Sniffing out children like hungry dogs."

"Hang on," interrupted Vinnie. "Does this mean you don't know how to get there either then?"

Gelda nodded, "That's right. We don't know the way; never privy to that information. But we knew it existed. However Vinnie, you are part of the Brotherhood and you have a better chance than any of finding the way."

Deflated, Vinnie whimpered, "I don't know the way. I really don't."

Mrs Muddles waddled over and held his face in her hands. "We know more than we did, Vinnie. We know that it's in the woods and we know that they will lead you there."

"Let's do this then!" exclaimed Vinnie as he grabbed his satchel and started towards the tunnel. Kitty and Lilana followed obediently, grabbing their bags, and filling them with bread from the table.

Gelda raced to the curtain cloaking the tunnel. "Wait, wait, you cannot be hasty. The Clodwalkers will be out there and will sniff you out the moment you step into the forest. You have to wait until night when they sleep."

Vinnie pushed forward. "We can't wait until then! The woods are dark enough in the day. By nightfall it will be impossible to see two steps in front of us. We will never make it."

Kitty looked thoughtful. "Vinnie, your father said never to be afraid of what you can't see. Maybe that means something. We cannot beat the Clodwalkers, so waiting it out is the only way. You said yourself to trust in your father."

Vinnie did trust in his father, and he knew that Kitty's acknowledgement of this was intended as some sort of apology. He nodded in acceptance and Kitty smiled.

"I have something that might help." Lilana reached into her bag and dragged out a brown paper bag. Untying the top, she pulled out some yellow and bright blue petals. "Petals from the Illuminas plant," she gestured, "Crush and mix with water and they should glow long enough to get us through the woods."

"Brilliant Lilana! Just brilliant!" exclaimed Vinnie grabbing her waist and spinning her around. "That's twice you've saved us, eh."

As Lilana ground the petals with water, Gelda prepared some bread and lumps of cheese wrapped in cloth. Vinnie nodded gratefully as he popped them in his satchel along with three flasks of water. Lilana spooned the petal mix into three empty jars and tied string around the lip to form a looped handle.

Mrs Muddles folded a blanket and stuffed it into Lilana's bag, tears welling up at the thought of them out there all alone. From her pocket she retrieved a small green package made of leaves tied with brown twine. She tapped Lilana on the shoulder and pressed the package into her hands. "I think this may be useful," she whispered. "It's Snorosa pollen."

Lilana gave Mrs Muddles a knowing look. "You used it on the Clodwalkers, right?"

Mrs Muddles nodded. "It can be very dangerous in the wrong hands, Lilana, but I know that it will be safe with you." Lilana pushed it down to the bottom of her bag and covered it with the blanket.

"I think it's time," suggested Kitty inspecting each of the four clocks scattered across the hollow. She watched as Lilana scrabbled around nervously for her bag, her vines almost invisible as they buried themselves into her blonde thicket. She eyed the tunnel nervously before padding slowly towards it.

Vinnie was stood at the entrance, petal lantern in hand and satchel thrown over his shoulder ready to take on the journey. Kitty joined them as Mrs Muddles threw her arms around them and squeezed them together as she wept. "Oh, be safe, please be safe."

Gelda peeled her away and gave them a reassuring smile. "They will be fine, Mrs Muddles, don't panic. Vinnie will lead the way." Vinnie stood looking as triumphant as he could, while gulping back the lump of responsibility lodged in his throat.

Gelda lifted the curtain. "Look after each other, be strong and stay together", she whispered. "Don't tell anyone we are here, or even that you saw us for that matter."

"Of course," answered Vinnie distracted by the dark tunnel ahead of him.

"Promise?" she asked.

"Not a word," replied Kitty.

They said their last goodbyes and headed on into the darkness of the tunnel. The petal lanterns illuminated their path with a blue glow that beamed ahead of them, as Gelda and Mrs Muddles watched the three small shadows disappear into the gloom.

Chapter 10: Lighting the Dark

As they stepped out of the hollow into the woods, the trees set alight with the blue glow of the lanterns. Branches twisted and flickered like flames, dancing from tree to tree as the children plodded anxiously through the woods. Clouds of blue vapour billowed up from the warm earth and settled at waist height, surrounding them in a misty ocean that tumbled across their path. It clung to their clothes, pulling them down to drown in its murky depths. They forged on against the tide, striding forward into the darkness.

They trundled through the woods, watching as tree after tree passed them by. The silent branches ushered them on as if through an endless photograph, unchanging and motionless.

After walking in silence for several hours, the lamps began to fade. The light began closing in on them as the path in front became less and less illuminated. Lilana began to feel uncertain and, as the darkness started closing in, she shuffled closer to Kitty.

Vinnie was trying to remain positive, but, as the lanterns faded, so did his optimism. His heart

87

sank as he watched Lilana and Kitty become increasingly nervous, glancing from side to side fearfully as they shuffled along the path.

"I'm sorry," he looked to the floor, "This is pointless. I have no idea where to go." He dropped to the ground and sat motionless, head in his hands, the lamp faintly glowing into the soil.

Kitty slumped down next to him dragging Lilana with her. Their lanterns placed together twinkled like the last glowing embers of a fire. "It's ok, Vinnie, it's not over," Kitty reassured. "We have come this far and it is no time to give up. We just need a moment to think." She pulled Lilana closer as the blue embers began to blacken.

Vinnie rubbed his head. "I just don't know anything more." He jiggled his lamp as the blue embers sparked. "I just want to see my family." He gave his lamp another shake as the embers flickered out one by one, and the darkness eventually swallowed them up.

The moon shone down through the leafless canopy, but Lilana couldn't even see her own hands as she hugged her ankles. Breathing slowly, she could smell the damp earth. She longed for the safety of her garden, as she dragged her fingers through the soil and inhaled deeply. When she opened her eyes, she saw a light jump across the ground in front of her. It skipped from her hand to her foot, bouncing again across the ground and landing to rest on Kitty's lap. "What's that?" Kitty leapt to her feet and shook her leg.

Lilana watched curiously as the flickering light moved forwards along the path into the darkness and then disappeared. She looked up at Vinnie who, oblivious to the situation, sat rubbing his head. "Stop!" she shouted. "What's that?" She pointed at his wrist where a white glint of light had appeared.

Motionless, Vinnie stared at his wrist as he reached up and pulled down his sleeve. A shaft of light streaked into the darkness, beaming from his periapt. "What the…?" Vinnie looked shocked. He moved his arm from side to side, waving it across his head. Wherever his arm was placed the beam of light was unyielding. It pointed in the same direction with the same furious glare.

"It's leading the way," Kitty laughed. "It's capturing the moonlight and shining it in the direction we need to go!"

Lilana jumped up. "The darkness is your friend, Vinnie, the darkness is your friend," she squealed as she danced around the extinguished lanterns.

"Let's go," ordered Vinnie as he raced onwards, arm outstretched as he ran towards the beam. Kitty and Lilana followed, sprinting after him. They stampeded through the forest, their feet thundering across the damp earth with renewed energy and sense of purpose. Hope drove them onward.

Breathless, they reached a clearing and the shaft of light disappeared as quickly as it had emerged. Replacing it came the familiar warm haze of lamplight from several small buildings scattered around a central green. Vinnie took off towards the smallest of the buildings as Kitty and Lilana stopped, slumping against the nearest tree, and gasping for air.

Vinnie threw open the wooden door and crashed into the house he called home.

Stunned, his mother dropped the pot she was filling and skidded through the spilled water to hold him. He sobbed warm tears into her scarf as she stroked his face gently and clutched him tighter. His father sprang up and skidded over to join them, surrounding them both in his strong embrace.

In the doorway, Kitty and Lilana watched silently and held hands more tightly than ever. It was just them now, and they knew it.

"Who's this?" Vinnie's father looked to the doorway.

Vinnie wiped his eyes briefly before heading to the doorway and pulling Kitty and Lilana into the room. He slammed the door behind them. "This is Kitty and Lilana, my friends from Elmsmere," he smiled at them in thanks, overwhelmed with the gratefulness he felt for their friendship. "I wouldn't be here without them."

Kitty stepped forward. "Nice to meet you Mr and Mrs Shadowsmith."

"Well, that's quite enough of that!" Mrs Shadowsmith smiled, "Mrs Shadowsmith indeed. I'm Raina and this is Elgor."

Elgor held out his hand and Kitty took it as he led them both to the Slump. Lilana snuggled down into the soft blankets and sipped on the Elmberry tea that Raina had been preparing before they had been interrupted. Vinnie sat between his parents, trapped tightly for fear of losing them again.

Elgor watched as his wife delighted in stroking Vinnie's hand and sniffing his hair, remembering the scent of him, and smiling. She had cried for weeks after he was taken; weeping at every meal; sobbing at every bedtime. This was the first week that she had not pined outwardly for their son. Although he did not doubt that she had been consumed with sadness and was mourning his loss, she had not shed a tear for days, and yesterday she had smiled.

His heavy heart beat loudly in his chest as he knew what was to come, and what it would do to his wife. They could not stay and there was nothing he could do to change that. Tomorrow they would need to leave.

Chapter 11: Home Sweet Home

Vinnie awoke and his heavy eyes came slowly into focus. On the floor, huddled together under a large woollen blanket lay Kitty and Lilana, breathing softly as they slept. He shuffled down to the end of the bed and slipped to the floor. He skirted along the four walls of his room, touching each and every object as he passed. He paused at the wooden periapts he had whittled as he sat watching his father craft his beautiful crystal creations for the children of the village. He smiled as he remembered how his father would chip and file each crystal into a magnificent beast, while he poked and prodded a branch until it looked almost like an animal, but not quite. His father would lift him into the sky and swing him around in celebration, praising him on his work, no matter how mis-shapen or crooked it looked.

Glancing once more at Kitty and Lilana, he smiled and tiptoed his way to the doorway. Skipping down the stairs towards the heavenly scent of oat Crumblers and Elmberry jam, he let his hand sweep along the bannister and across the wall, taking in every inch of the home he loved.

His mother was busying herself at the oven. Covered head to toe in the white dust of oat flour, she hummed and wiggled as she danced with joy, kneading the Crumbler dough to the rhythm of her song.

Vinnie crept slowly towards her and grabbed her shoulders as she let out a squeal. She spun around and batted his hands away. A cloud of dust puffed into the air as they giggled.

Vinnie grabbed a hot cup of Elmberry tea and snuggled into the Slump. "Where's Father?" he asked, slurping loudly.

"You haven't been gone long enough to have lost your manners!" Raina grimaced as Vinnie wiped his mouth on his sleeve. "Your father's finishing some work. Beautiful it is. You should go and see." Vinnie slurped the final drips of his Elmberry tea as his mother chased him out with her disapproving glare.

Elgor, deep in thought, was polishing an elegant crystal periapt shaped into the perfect teardrop. The girl who was to have it could harness the power of water. Although Elgor could have made a majestic wave or a powerful waterfall, he knew that tears would be the water she would find hardest to control. He felt Vinnie's presence before he saw him and he turned to see his strong, clever son and smiled. "It's so good to have you back," he whispered. His smile dropped as he looked to the ground.

Confused Vinnie crossed the room to hug him, "Come on Father, this is a good thing. I escaped. I'm here; home where I should be."

Elgor stepped back, keeping hold of Vinnie's shoulders. "You will never know how proud I feel right now. How that pride swells inside me, holding me taller and making me stronger. You have been courageous and fierce. I couldn't have asked for more than this in a son. But you cannot stay here."

Vinnie stumbled backwards, staring in disbelief. "What? Of course I can. I hid before and I'll hide again."

Elgor placed his hand gently on Vinnie's arm. "They will come for you and they will find you, Vinnie. Your gift is strong now and they will feel it.

Do you honestly believe that Elmsmere will let this go? This is the first place they will come looking, and they will find you. You will need to find somewhere safe to go. Somewhere safe to hide… Somewhere to make a new home."

Tears dripped silently from Elgor's chin and his heart broke in his chest as he watched his son silently cry as he had done as a baby.

Elgor pulled him into his chest and squeezed him tightly. "Before you left you had your mother and me and that was enough. You lived an invisible life, a silent life, and, in truth, a lonely life. You have friends now. Great friends that rely on you. You are strong and fearless, and they need you. Even if you come back now, you would not be content with the silence and isolation. You have changed for the better and have become the boy you should always have been. There is no going back."

Vinnie inhaled the musky scent of hot metal and leather from his father's overalls and wept, but he knew his father was right. As much as he had felt imprisoned at Elmsmere, he had made friends and gained a voice. And although he missed his family, returning to silence and invisibility, was in reality returning home to a prison he hadn't realised existed. Besides, he had to admit that Lilana and Kitty had played on his mind today; where would they go? How would they get there? Would they be safe? Pangs of guilt interrupted his thoughts.

Vinnie pulled away from his father, wiped his eyes, and took a deep breath, "What about Mother?"

Elgor sighed, "She knows, Vinnie. She knows. She is baking a feast for you to take with you. And don't worry – she is stronger than you think."

Vinnie and Elgor laughed as they strolled in, grabbing an oat Crumbler, followed by a playful slap and tut from Raina. They snuggled together on the Slump and ate silently.

Raina gave Vinnie a reassuring look, patting his hand as she smiled, "I'm proud of you. You need to take those girls and find somewhere safe to stay and not worry about us. Can you think of anywhere?"

Vinnie paused, "We did stay with some Groggles," he noted, "I guess we could go back there."

"Wow, Groggles!" exclaimed Elgor. "I thought they'd all been sent to the mines."

"Morning." Lilana and Kitty appeared at the foot of the stairs, sleepy and slow. They accepted Raina's invitation for oat Crumblers and Elmberry tea and dropped into the Slump as discussions of their departure continued.

Lilana listened to the chatter, anxiously taking in the details of the plan while Kitty nodded enthusiastically. Moving on tonight, the Seekers were coming, staying together, finding somewhere safe for them to stay, maybe with Gelda and Mrs Muddles…

"What about Iris?" The room fell silent as realisation washed over Vinnie's face. They had forgotten about Iris! Lilana shuffled in her seat, "I need to find Iris."

Vinnie and Kitty exchanged glances, "The first thing we need to do Lilana is find a safe place to be. The Groggles can help us with that. They've managed to stay hidden, and maybe they can show us how," Kitty spoke reassuringly. "Then we will have a base and we can search for Iris. The Groggles will be sure to help."

Lilana smiled and Kitty reached out to hold her hand. "You have saved us more than once, Lilana. We will never forget that."

Elgor bounded up onto his feet. "What's that?" he demanded pointing at Kitty's wrist where her Periapt dangled, the gold cord swinging it from left to right. "Who are you?"

Kitty rolled her eyes and pulled her sleeve down to cover her periapt, "Why do people keep asking me that?"

"Because you have a royal periapt, I expect," replied Elgor, grabbing her wrist. "Did you steal it?"

"No!" Kitty looked furious. "I'm not a thief. I've had it since birth." She snatched her arm away from Elgor.

He pulled it back. "Let me see it." Kitty grabbed the periapt, pulling it off her wrist, and threw it at Elgor. "Here have it. It means nothing anyway. It's not like I have a gift to go with it."

Elgor took a step back glaring at the periapt, turning it over in his hands, "What are you talking about? Your gift is strong, I feel it every time you enter a room."

Kitty stared, open mouthed. *He could feel it?* "Do you know what it is?" she whimpered. "Can you tell me what my gift is?"

Elgor looked bewildered. "What? You don't know?" he asked as she dropped down into the Slump. She shook her head and he watched the sadness well up in her eyes.

Sitting down next to her, he raised his hand, took a deep breath and gently touched her forehead. His face lit up as the warmth filled his toes, creeping up his legs, slowly filling his belly, and rising up until his cheeks flushed with the heat of her gift.

She watched as he grinned for a few moments before a look of confusion crossed his face. His hand dropped to his side. "I don't know what to say Kitty. Your gift is from the light, that's for certain, but it's strange… I can't tell what it is."

"Come on Father, try again!" Vinnie jeered, "You can tell her, I know you can."

100

Elgor hated disappointing his son. He placed his hand back on Kitty's head, but nothing had changed. He sensed the warmth of her gift, he felt the light within her, but he couldn't visualise the gift itself. He shook his head, "I'm so sorry, it's never happened to me before."

Lilana smiled at Kitty. "It will come Kitty. At least you know you have one." Kitty nodded in agreement. She did feel better knowing she had the periapt for a reason.

Elgor reached into the pocket of his overalls and pulled out a little black pot. "This periapt will draw attention to you Kitty, unwanted attention. I don't know where you got it or why you have it, but it needs to be hidden." He unscrewed the lid of the pot, plunged his finger in, and smeared a black shiny sludge across the periapt and its cord. "This will dry in no time and it will look just like the periapt of a chief's daughter; much less attention-grabbing." Kitty retied the periapt around her wrist and covered it with her sleeve.

Raina brushed the crumbs from the table into her hands and trundled towards the kitchen, dusting them into the bin as she passed. "Let's have some Bungle Pie," she suggested as she opened the oven. The smell of sweet Bungle berries wafted through the room. Lilana took a deep breath, inhaling the sickly scent; she closed her eyes.

"Shhh!" snapped Elgor. "Quiet."

"What?" bellowed Vinnie as Elgor glared at him angrily. "Shhh."

The sound of air rushing past the window seemed to alarm Elgor. Vinnie tutted, but the sound seemed to escalate in strength and had a strange rhythmic quality to it. It whooshed and whirred; its speed remaining the same. The sound became stronger and stronger, until the tree outside began to rustle along to the pulsating, whipping of the wind.

"Get upstairs," ordered Elgor. "Move now, quickly. It's them, it's the Seekers." Kitty headed for the stairs dragging a startled Lilana with her, Vinnie scuttled behind them. As he rushed into his room, he carefully closed the door, just as they heard the dreaded knock.

Chapter 12: Introducing Jasper Chatterwick

Vinnie gestured to Kitty, pointing at the window, as he comforted Lilana who had hidden her face in her hands. Mumblings and murmurings from downstairs crept up the staircase. Lilana shuddered as the conversation below became louder and more frantic. She clamped her hands over her ears.

Kitty tiptoed across the room and peeked through the corner of the window. Immediately below the window sat a wooden cart, attached by two sets of reins to a small, brown, furry creature. It had little brown ears that twitched as flies spun and twisted around its head. It scuffed at the ground in irritation. At the back corner of the cart, the Seekers had tied a small boy. He sat. Hunched. Motionless.

She beckoned them over. Pointing down to the cart she whispered, "The cart is our only option. There's a boy in it. I'm not convinced that the creature pulling it will get us very far, but I don't think we have a choice."

Vinnie scoffed. "That thing! Really?! You've got to be kidding me!"

"And your plan is?" Kitty asked.

103

Vinnie shook his head as he pulled the handle to open the window. He clambered over the window ledge, dangled his legs out backwards, clinging to the ledge with his fingertips, and then dropped onto the cart with a thud. "Come on," he mouthed to Lilana and Kitty.

Lilana shook her head back and forth mouthing, "No. No. No." Kitty pushed her towards the window, pointing to the room below, and shrugging her shoulders. Lilana shivered as she pulled herself over the ledge. She clung to it, her eyes closed tightly as she muttered, "I can't let go. I can't let go." Kitty paced in front of the window willing her to drop.

As the voices below got louder, Kitty paced more quickly and, in a moment of frustration, she reached over and peeled Lilana's fingertips from the edge. Lilana let out a squeal as she tumbled into the cart. Kitty ran across the room to the bed and grabbed Lilana's bag. Racing to the window, she threw her legs over the ledge and jumped, landing feet first.

Thrusting the bag at Lilana, she grabbed the reins. She started to shake them up and down urging the creature to move. Its ears flickered but its feet stayed rooted in the earth. "Come on, come on," she uttered. "Move animal, move." Vinnie threw his arms into the air and shook his head, while Lilana looked on with her arms wrapped tightly around her legs.

From the corner of her eye, Kitty caught sight of movement. She turned to see the boy in the corner, whom in all honesty she had forgotten about. His mouth had been covered with a large cloth that had been tied tightly around his head. His arms and legs were also tied to a post at the back of the cart. He was shuffling his whole body and blinking uncontrollably. He kept looking down and shaking his head violently, sending his hair into a dancing frenzy. He was trying to move his mouth. His brown eyes widened in frustration. Kitty grabbed the cloth from his mouth.

"Finally!" he moaned. "Blimey, you took long enough. Now grab something; anything and hold tight… very tight."

"What do you…?" Vinnie started.

"Just grab something now!" the boy shouted in reply.

105

The boy turned towards the front of the cart and began to growl and bark. The brown creature shuffled and its ears perked up. The boy growled louder, barked four times, and let out a howl that shook the cart and the children in it. At this, the animal began to stomp and its back began to move independently of the rest of its body. Its fur started to lift and its shoulders seemed to uncurl and unravel, until two enormous brown furry wings unfolded, stretching outwards and upwards. It began to shuffle and, as it lifted its wings, the boy shouted, "Hold tight!" The familiar rhythmic whoosh of air, lifted the cart high off the ground. It jolted forward into the woods to the frantic cries of the Seekers below.

As the cart glided through the air, Kitty caught her breath and turned to the boy who was growling quietly to the majestic beast as they soared through the air. "I'm Kitty" she announced, "And this is Lilana and Vinnie."

"Jasper Chatterwick," replied the boy, "Ten-time escapee, well actually 11, thanks to you. Can you help me with these ropes?" Kitty untied his hands and legs and he rubbed at his wrists and

106

winced. "They tie them tighter every time I'm sure." Stumbling forward, he sat behind their furry pilot and gently stroked its side in thanks.

The cart was steady now, gently bobbing up and down along with the pulsing beat of the wings. The air rushed past and stirred Kitty's hair into a frenzy. She drooped her arm around Lilana's shoulders and pulled her into her side, rubbing her arm reassuringly.

Vinnie stared out behind them, "I didn't get to say goodbye." He looked to the floor and back into the forest, his eyes searching for a final glimpse of the family he had lost for a second time. His body wilted as he moaned softly to himself.

The sleepy sun closed its eyes as it snuggled to rest behind the dark night sky. Lilana shifted up closer to Kitty. "I'm hungry, Kitty," she sighed as she looked across to Vinnie, "We didn't manage to bring the food your mother baked; such a shame." Vinnie nodded in silent acknowledgement.

Jasper jumped up and strolled to the end of the cart. "Don't you worry about that!" he laughed. "Those Seekers are a greedy bunch and they do not do things by halves!" Reaching down he lifted a latch and pulled up a panel on the floor of the cart. Reaching in he dragged out two bags and a pile of fur and wool blankets which he shoved towards Kitty and Lilana. "Tuck in."

Snuggled in fur and wool they feasted on Oat Crumblers, Elmberry tarts, dried fruit, stuffed bread and spiced meats. With full bellies and tired eyes, they snoozed until morning.

Jasper awoke to the hushed tones of confusion and anger. Vinnie seemed agitated and was tapping his fingers rapidly on the side of the cart. "Well, clearly we have passed the Groggles and have absolutely no idea where we are. Safety was what we were heading for and what have we got. Well, in all honesty, who knows where we are? Come on, where are we going? Either of you? Anyone?"

"I know." Jasper stretched his arms upwards and yawned. "We are going home. Well, to his home." He nodded to the front of the cart. "He will take us to the Pelnack Plains, home of the Pelnacks, and where he was taken from his family."

Vinnie shook his head. "Great, that's great. Couldn't you have asked him to drop us somewhere useful?! No?"

Jasper stretched again, his yawn seeming to further irritate an already ruffled Vinnie. "Maybe it's best if we get acquainted, eh. You tell me your story. I'll tell you mine. Might help us think more clearly?" Jasper broke some stuffed bread into pieces and handed them around the cart, smiling and nodding.

Vinnie softened. "Fine," he replied and told the story of their escape from Elmsmere.

Jasper was captivated with their story and seemed ready to burst at any minute, desperate to interject. When Vinnie had finished, Jasper launched into his own story, excited by the similarities between them. He came from an Academy much like them, called Widowsworth Academy for the Gifted. He had escaped several times, but the Seekers always found him. On his twelfth birthday, the Seekers came to the Academy and took him.

At this point Lilana jumped up. "Where did they take you? Where? Is it nearby?" Her voice juddered in desperation.

Jasper stopped, "Do you not know?" The three friends shook their heads and Jasper took a deep breath. "When you come of age it is time for you to walk your path. Monelda's words not mine," he grumbled. "They take you to Melgron Barracks where they ask you about your gift and the Seekers evaluate you. There are two pathways, basically jobs that Monelda deems you fit for. You don't get paid and don't get a choice. You will either join her army or work in the Regent Stronghold; neither of which I wanted to do. They wanted me to join her army, talk to animals and force them to do her bidding… Hence escape number 11."

Kitty grunted. "Well, what now then? What's your plan?"

"There was talk at Melgron Barracks of a safe place called The Hidden Haven where children like us can have our own lives and that's where I'm heading. Come with me?" Jasper looked at his new friends with hope. "We will be better together I'm sure. Safety in numbers and all that!"

"I need to find my sister," Lilana uttered. "Iris deserves to be safe. I want her to be safe. I need to find her."

"Iris… hmmm. I met an Iris!" Jasper cried. "She went to the Regent's Stronghold. Perfect lookout they said, and could have fitted in the army too, but she was too… Well, army types tend to be darker in nature."

Lilana's eyes filled with tears. She couldn't decide if she was happy or sad so just wept all the same. "I need to get her," she sobbed.

Jasper clapped his hands, "Now this is becoming an adventure!"

Vinnie rolled his eyes and shook his head, "Great. Off to the Regents Stronghold to risk our lives and then into the unknown to find this Hidden Haven that may or may not exist. Sounds like a great plan."

Jasper jumped to his feet. "Come on Vinnie, mate, what other plans have you got for this afternoon," he laughed.

Kitty smiled and hopped up to join him. "I'm in!" she declared, dragging Lilana up with her, who beamed at the prospect of finding Iris.

"I don't have much choice then do I," grumbled Vinnie. "Where's this Pelnack fella taking us then?"

Jasper scruffed the Pelnack's fur and purred at him. "Lucky for us Monelda's Stronghold isn't far from Pelnack Plains. A day or two's walk at the most."

Vinnie rolled his eyes again. "How very handy," he uttered under his breath as he looked out into the cloudy horizon and groaned.

Chapter 13: The Great Race

Vinnie watched as Kitty exited the cart. Jasper held her by her fingertips, and lowered her to the ground.

He wasn't jealous exactly. Of course not; what even was there to be jealous of? So he can talk to animals, wow wee. We all have gifts.

It was just the constant chattering throughout the journey, talking about their lives and what they could have been, and the tragedy of having it all taken away. How they were going to find this Hidden Haven and it was all going to be fabulous. Kitty seemed so at ease and even thanked him for saving them over and over and over. It was soooo boring. No wonder Lilana slept for the whole journey. What was she thanking him for anyway?! He was tied to the cart that WE released him from, and Vinnie could have given that Pelnack a mighty smack on the backside and it would have flown off. One thing he was sure of was that Jasper Chatterwick did not save HIS life.

Lilana plonked down next to Vinnie and shook her head. Her hair came alive as each vine-like tendril awoke and shuddered. They wiggled

113

eventually settling, nuzzled into her neck. "Is everything ok?" she asked, recognising the sadness in his eyes, "Do you miss them?"

Vinnie's stomach lurched with guilt as he realised that he was so busy worrying about Jasper that he had forgotten about his mother and father. He lowered his head and let out a breathy sigh. "Just for a minute, Lilana, I had forgotten how much I miss them, and if I'm honest it felt good. And now, well, now I feel guilty for having such a thought."

Lilana reached over to pluck some yellow moss from the ground at Vinnie's feet. "I will be forever thankful to you Vinnie for bringing me here. I know it was no small decision you made to leave your family for us." Vinnie turned as she stuffed the moss into her pocket. "Hittle Moss has fantastic healing properties," she explained as she turned to follow his stare. Kitty and Jasper were admiring the view; Jasper describing its beauty with his hands as Kitty nodded in agreement. "It is beautiful isn't it?" Lilana smiled, "Like a green ocean rising and dipping to the horizon."

Vinnie stood up and brushed the moss from his legs. "We better hope we don't drown in it, I suppose," he snapped as he wandered towards the others. "Come on Lilana, we had better go and thank our saviour."

The Pelnack Plains were a sea of greens and yellows undulating in all directions, the crest of each wave being nibbled by a little furry Pelnack. Kitty shut her eyes and welcomed in the tranquillity and the sense of freedom she had never had. She watched as Jasper untethered their Pelnack pilot. He thundered off into the distance, leaving a spray of green moss in his wake. At least one of them had made it home, she thought, as she admired the joy on Jasper's face.

Jasper understood how lost Kitty felt, having been abandoned by his parents and having no other family. Vinnie had his family, Lilana had Iris, and Kitty had no one. Jasper understood her and she needed that.

He came bounding towards her, dragging Lilana and Vinnie behind him. "Who's for some fun?" he asked with a smile. "We deserve some fun, don't we?" Lilana nodded and Kitty jumped up clapping her hands. "Let's do this!" Jasper shouted as he ran towards a small burrow. "Follow me!"

115

Standing by the entrance to the burrow, Lilana shuffled from foot to foot, anxious with expectation. The burrow was clearly that of an animal and, although she was certain that Jasper wouldn't put them in any sort of danger, his sense of danger and her's were very different things. She stared into the dark tunnel and shuddered. Kitty however was hopping from foot to foot in excitement, her eyes wide as she stared into the tunnel. Vinnie lingered at the back, his mind seemingly elsewhere.

Jasper cupped his hands over his mouth and made a clicking sound. He scuffed his feet on the ground creating a cloud of dust that swirled around them. Vinnie coughed loudly and shook his head. The clicking got louder and Jasper began to squeak and squeal, scuffing his feet more rapidly. The dust swirled and whipped around them and then, suddenly, he stopped.

An eerie silence beckoned as the dust cloud began to drop and the children looked at each other blankly. Jasper began to smile as a low buzz drifted from the burrow and the ground beneath them vibrated as it got louder and louder. The buzz

116

became a frantic scuttling sound that increased in speed until the burrow exploded onto the plain. An enormous, shelled creature raced out bundling towards Jasper. It stopped sharply in front of him. He rubbed its shell as the dust cloud rained over it.

As tall as Jasper, its domed, brown shell was spattered in orange spots. Dangling below the shell were hundreds of spindly legs that moved continuously even when the creature was stationary. Perched on top of the shell were two thick, black stems topped with bright green eyes.

Jasper grasped one of the stems like a handle and swung himself up onto the creature. His legs wrapped around the shell. He grabbed both eye stems and rubbed them like he was greeting an old friend. "This is Poppin," he announced. "He is a Popkin Bug and he just loves to be ridden; luckily for you so do his friends."

No sooner had he spoken than the ground began to vibrate and shake as three Popkin Bugs thundered out of the burrow and skidded to a halt. "Jump on!" Jasper shouted.

Kitty swung herself up onto the nearest Popkin and grabbed its eye stems. "Woohoo!" she screeched. "Come on guys, what's the hold up?"

Lilana looked nervously towards the smallest Popkin who lolloped towards her. It nudged her gently and rubbed up against her, setting her at ease. She grabbed its eye stem and launched herself up onto its shell, wobbling and grabbing at the other eye stem to settle herself. Vinnie reluctantly grasped an eye stem and spun up onto an anxious-looking Popkin as it shuffled on the spot.

"Let's race to those trees over there at the end of the meadow," Jasper hollered. "Last one makes the lunch!"

"You're on!" replied Vinnie. If there was one thing he was good at it was moving quickly and Jasper needed to be taken down a peg or two. "How do we get these things started?" he asked.

"Squeeze your legs," replied Jasper as he squeezed the shell of Poppin gently and moved slowly forward. "The left stem tells them to turn left; the right stem to turn right. Simple really." They lined up next to each other, the spindly legs swirling up a ground fog of dust. Jasper counted down, "Three, two, one… Go!"

Vinnie nudged his heels into the shell of his steed and grabbed on as he shot forward, crashing over the mossy earth. Pulling on the right eye stem, they swerved to the right onto some flatter ground, avoiding the mounded plains ahead. "Aha!" he shouted, pleased with his smart thinking. Jasper, with the same idea, zoomed up beside him, grinning as he rushed past. Vinnie dug his heels in harder and he sidled up next to Jasper, who was slightly ahead.

Kitty zipped forward, swinging left and right, avoiding the mossy peaks and gasping with joy as her dark hair whipped in the breeze from side to side as she changed direction. Exhilarated by the rush of air, she squeezed harder and surged forward.

Lilana had decided that if she wanted to eat well this afternoon it was probably best if she cooked. This meant that she could lose the race and enjoy a gentle amble across the plains. She made her way to the side of the meadow where some familiar plants were growing. Her new Popkin friend made her the perfect height to pick the nuts and berries she needed to make a delicious meal. Muddling along she popped a berry into her mouth and smiled as she watched Vinnie and Jasper scuffle for first place.

With the trees in sight Vinnie forged forward giving himself a firm lead "Ha ha!" he laughed as Jasper dropped back and swerved to the left.

Confused, Vinnie turned to see a huge mossy heap rising up in front of him. He grabbed the left eye stem and leaned as far left as he could, squeezing his eyes shut. The Popkin shot sideways narrowly missing the mound, but crashed like an angry crab across the plain and bowled into Jasper and Poppin. Vinnie watched as Jasper flew into the air and tumbled across the ground, skidding through the mud and landing with a thud at the base of a tree.

Kitty slid off her Popkin and raced over to the tree where Jasper lay motionless. "Jasper, Jasper are you ok?" she asked, gently pulling his hair away from his face. Poppin nudged at his legs and he groaned quietly. "Jasper!" Kitty gave a sigh of relief. She turned to face Vinnie who had arrived, closely followed by Lilana. "What were you thinking?" she snapped. "He's hurt! You just smashed into him."

Vinnie looked worried. "I'm sorry Kitty, it was an accident. I just didn't see the hill." He saw Jasper and felt the guilt wash over him. "I'm so sorry."

Lilana held his shoulder as she passed. "It's ok, Vinnie, you were racing and it all just went a bit far. It's not your fault." Kitty glared in disagreement.

Lilana knelt beside Jasper and looked him up and down. His eyes were open and he smiled. "My leg hurts," he whimpered.

She pulled up the leg of his trousers to reveal a large gash just below his knee. Rummaging in her bag, she found a small clump of Hittle Moss which she pressed into the wound and tied in place with some torn cloth. Jasper winced as she tightened the cloth and he shuffled to sit up, leaning against the tree. "Drink this." Lilana passed him a jar filled with water, peppered with Nora flowers. Gulping it down, Jasper smiled in thanks and closed his eyes.

He awoke to the smell of hot broth and oat Crumblers. Kitty spotted his eyes open and rushed over. "How are you feeling?" she asked.

"I'm fine Kitty, don't worry, honestly. Whatever Lilana did is working, it feels better already," Jasper tried to stand but wobbled back down to the ground and drooped against the tree.

Lilana stirred the broth and began dishing it into jars. "You will need a few days to recover properly," she instructed. "Maybe tomorrow we can think about our next steps."

Jasper shook his head. "We can't wait until tomorrow!" he exclaimed. "We need to leave now and use the night to shroud us. We can leave straight after dinner."

Lilana handed him his broth and giggled. "This is breakfast, Jasper, you have slept for 18 hours. I gave you some Nora flowers to ease the pain and help you sleep. It IS tomorrow."

"What?" Jasper looked agitated and dragged himself to stand. "You drugged me! What were you thinking? We need to get to the Stronghold and don't have time for napping and sitting about. You idiot!"

Vinnie, silent until now, jumped up. "Hang on a minute, Jasper, you watch yourself. She was trying to help you. What you should be saying is thank you, not insulting her." He pulled Lilana towards him protectively.

Jasper, more agitated than ever, hobbled towards the woods. "Thanks for putting me to sleep against my will. I don't think so."

Vinnie grabbed Lilana's bag, waved it in the air, and thrust it towards Jasper. "If it wasn't for the stuff in this bag you wouldn't even be walking my friend. You want to show some gratitude. Besides, you seemed to think we had plenty of time for racing around on your little bug chums. Now we don't have time to rest and eat. Make your mind up."

Kitty raced to help Jasper, grabbing his arm to steady him. "Well maybe if you didn't turn it into some ridiculous competition, Vinnie, we wouldn't be in this situation," she uttered. "It was you that got us into this mess!"

"Me? Me! It was Jasper here that wanted to race. I was just joining in all the fun he was telling us to have!"

123

Kitty huffed, "Oh please, you've been in a grump since we got here. You can't take your upset out on Jasper. He saved us." Vinnie's face reddened. His eyes bulged as he stepped toward Kitty. He felt a pull on his arm.

"Let's go for a walk," suggested Lilana tugging at his sleeve. "We could all do with a minute to calm down." She led him off into the woods and Kitty watched as they disappeared into the undergrowth.

Vinnie slumped down against a large tree dropping his head into his hands. Lilana joined him, leaning in, and slipping her arm behind him reassuringly to give him a gentle squeeze. He sighed as he felt a strange cold breeze sweep up from behind him. He turned to see a look of uncertainty in Lilana's eyes. He grabbed her hand as he realised that the solid wood behind his back had disappeared. He toppled backwards and gasped as they both tumbled downwards into the darkness.

124

Chapter 14: The Crystals are all Mine

Lilana lay, beached on the sodden earth, gasping for air. The only sound was her own heavy panting. She pulled the wet strands of hair away from her face in an attempt to view her surroundings. Still submerged in total darkness, she shuddered and closed her eyes. "Vinnie?" she exhaled. "Vinnie? Are you here?" With no answer forthcoming she sank into the earth, her body weighted with fear. Suddenly, she felt something cold and wet clasp her wrist and she screamed, slapping it and scuffling across the ground.

"Ow!" Vinnie jumped to his feet, clinging to his fingers. "What did you do that for?" He towered over Lilana, who stared at him for a moment, before erupting into laughter. Her hair flitting about as if tittering along with her.

Vinnie was covered from head to toe in brown soil, broken twigs and prickly leaves. Outlined by the darkness, his shadow poked into the air like an angry hedgehog. Lilana's relief on finding him turned to immediate and absolute amusement. She giggled and squealed as she rummaged around in her bag for her last jar of

125

Illumina Petals. "I don't have any water," she managed to mutter between chuckles.

"What?" Vinnie snapped, "Your priority is having a drink? We have just fallen through a tree trunk into some kind of… Well, who knows what, actually, and you want a drink!"

As he spoke, he shuffled around flinging the twigs and leaves from his hair into the shadows. Lilana held her breath to stifle the laughter, but it erupted again. She snorted and gasped with glee. "I'm so sorry," she smirked. "You look ridiculous, Vinnie!"

"Well, I'm glad you find this all so funny, Lilana."

Seeing he was upset, Lilana handed him the jar. "We need water for the Illumina Petals. Then we can have a good look around and find a way out."

Vinnie unscrewed the lid, took a breath and spat several times into the jar. Then, plucking a twig from his hair, he stirred the contents until a faint blue glow beamed across the earth at his feet. He raised the jar to find Lilana's face, twisted in disgust. "What? You wanted water, I gave you water! Not so funny now, eh," he laughed.

Pulling Lilana to her feet, he surveyed their surroundings. They seemed to be trapped in some sort of cave. The walls were formed of rock and earth, stippled with shiny stones. Vinnie stepped towards the wall, running his hands over the rock. "Periapt crystals," he mused as he thought of his father.

Lilana joined him, "They are beautiful," she beamed as she ran her fingers over a small clear crystal. "Do you think we are in the mines?" she asked.

"Well, the edge of one probably, judging by these walls," Vinnie answered. "These crystals are small. Useless for periapts. They have probably already mined the larger ones. Let's hope it's an empty mine and we can find a way out." He lifted the jar to view their entrance tunnel, a large, dark hole hovering above them. "We are not getting out of there," he mused.

Lilana began feeling her way along the walls, searching for an exit. "Here, Vinnie, over here!" she cried. What had seemed like a wall was actually a passageway of some sort.

Vinnie dashed across the room, "Lilana, that's brilliant. Well done. Now let's see where it leads."

Lilana held her hand up to stop Vinnie is his path. "I am not going anywhere with you looking liking that," she grinned, as she dusted the soil from his arms and picked the leaves and sticks from his hair. "Much better," she uttered, strolling off into the passageway.

They wandered on, tunnel after tunnel, passage after passage. They all looked the same: dark and never ending. Lilana, weary and hungry, stopped to lean against the wall and catch her breath. "I'm worried," she muttered. "It's dark and cold and we have no food. I'm scared."

"So you should be!" The voice sliced through the darkness and Lilana turned to see a familiar figure striding towards them. "Well, well, well, if it's not wimpy Lilana. Now you are the last person I expected to see down here." Lilana's hair quivered as she recognised the figure as Chordata Weavil. She was closely followed as always by several small, sneering minions. "I see you are still talking to yourself Lilana. That's what happens when your only friends are plants, I guess," she jeered. The minions chuckled.

Lilana glanced to her side; Vinnie had disappeared.

"I fell through a tree," Lilana mumbled. "I was looking for berries." She looked to the ground. She was not a good liar.

"Oh, Lilana," Chordata taunted, "Do you honestly think that I'm that stupid. You and your little friends are wanted by the Regent and handing you in will help rise me up the ranks, I'm sure of that."

She slid up close to Lilana, pausing to listen to the air around them. "Where are they, Lilana? Your so-called friends. Did they push you down that tunnel?" Her warm breath tickled the hair on Lilana's neck. "Or are they here somewhere, hiding like the cowards they are."

"Chordata! Chordata!" There was a large thump as Chordata turned to see her three minions slump to the ground. Rolling her eyes, she turned to face Lilana as she felt her feet being swept from beneath her. She crashed into the wall and tumbled to the ground.

"Run Lilana!" shouted Vinnie as he thundered towards her. "Move now!" Lilana turned and started to run down the dark tunnel, sprinting towards the nearest exit. Her legs, swift at first, began to slow, refusing to move as quickly as she urged them. Her arms followed, preferring to remain stationary at her side rather than surge forward as she wished. Her legs felt heavy and tired and eventually refused to move at all. She stood motionless like a statue. She heard stomping footsteps pacing towards her.

Chordata appeared in front of her, grinning as she brushed the dust from her hands. "So it turns out that I have quite the gift. I always managed to get people to do what I want, sort of convinced them with my mind. In my time at Melgron Barracks I was shown just exactly what I am capable of. You see I can take over a person's nervous system. Brain, spine, muscles. All of it. I can stop them in their tracks. You've found that already." She laughed to herself and shook her head. "I will leave your little friend here paralysed

130

and alone if you don't appear," she shouted into the darkness. A dark, Vinnie shaped shadow revealed itself in the distance.

Lilana tried to speak but her throat tightened and she coughed. "Speech too, I'm afraid," Chordata bragged as she strolled past to shake her henchman awake. "Get up and chain them," she ordered.

Lilana and Vinnie dragged their tethered feet through the dirt. Attached to their left foot was a small boulder, which was fused to a metal chain. Lilana flinched as the metal dug into her ankle with each step. Her eyes began to water.

Vinnie watched Lilana as she wept. Helpless and guilt-ridden his shoulders sagged. Chordata marched on; an army ant dressed head to toe in scarlet linen; her once wild red hair now tamed into a neat bun. She turned to give Vinnie a venomous look. He felt his spine tingle and tighten as she smirked. She turned away. What was he going to do? How was he going to get them out of this? It wasn't just Lilana, it was Kitty too. She didn't know she was being hunted and he had to warn her. She also had no idea what had happened to

131

them. She might think that they had abandoned her and left her with Jasper. She was his first friend, his best friend, and he would never leave her. Never.

The corridor began to widen slightly as they walked, slowly opening up and becoming lighter with each step. The thuds of their feet plodding through the earth were joined by muffled voices, and a clanging sound that rattled down the walls. The noise became louder and louder. Vinnie began to realise that the mine was not abandoned as he had hoped.

The passageway ended in an enormous cave that stretched further than Vinnie could see, and reached up into a black sky of rock, twinkling with tiny crystals. The walls were crawling with Groggles, tied at the waist with ropes and hanging precariously against the rock. They held pickaxes that they swung towards the damp stone walls, clanging and clunking as stones and crystals showered down to the floor. Groggles scampered across the ground, collecting the debris and sorting it into baskets which were being lifted on to platforms. The platforms when full were hoisted up into the darkness, returning empty a few moments later. All of this was being overseen by an army of red soldiers.

The Groggles were dressed in brown trousers and thin, white vests. They looked tired. Covered in dust and dirt, some struggled to lift their pickaxes, or stopped briefly to rub their backs before being barked at to continue. Not a smile amongst them, they slogged on in silence.

Vinnie and Lilana were ushered into a large cavern that had been sectioned off from the rest of the cave. It had thick metal bars extending from floor to ceiling. A small metal door clanked shut behind them as they were shoved inside. Chordata rested her face between two bars and smirked.

"Yet another failed escape for you then Vinnie," she sniped. "Regent Monelda will be so thrilled when she knows I've captured you."

"What does she want with us?" Vinnie asked. "We are no-ones, of no significance to her."

Chordata shook her head and shrugged, "Beats me why she wants you. I mean you're as pathetic as these Groggles if you ask me. Anyway, you will be fed with the rest of them later. Then we will take you off to the Stronghold in the morning."

Vinnie grabbed the bars. With his face close to Chordata's, he snarled at her, "You will regret this Chordata!"

Stepping back, she laughed and pointed into the corner of the cavern, "Oh please, Vinnie, look at the pair of you! How are you going to make ME regret anything?"

Vinnie turned to see Lilana scrunched into the corner, shuddering and weeping. He felt his spine tingle as he turned to Chordata, who waved and walked away.

Vinnie rushed over to Lilana and wrapped his arms around her. "We will get out of here Lilana, I promise." Snuggled together, they drifted into sleep.

Chapter 15: Another Great Escape

Lilana felt a nudge as she yawned and stretched her arms. Opening her eyes, she gasped and jumped to her feet. "Vinnie, Vinnie, wake up!"

Vinnie came to with a start, banging his head on the wall. He moaned, "Oh, blimey, you made me jump, Lilana! Ow! What is …?"

He stopped mid-sentence as he came to understand Lilana's urgency. Stood around them, shoulder to shoulder were hundreds of Groggles, all looking accusingly at Lilana and Vinnie.

"Well, that's just great," huffed a small Groggle with a particularly lumpy nose. "We hardly get enough food as it is; and they are huge. Enormous in fact. They will eat a lot. And where will they sleep? We just about fit in here. It's ridiculous."

The Groggles jeered amongst themselves and began muttering and complaining loudly. The lumpy-nosed Groggle became agitated, "I suggest we don't feed them; I'm not willing to go hungry for the sake of some scrawny little children. What do these people ever do for us?"

The jeering became louder and louder and Lilana started to panic, retreating into the corner

135

and covering her ears. Vinnie grabbed her hand. "Stop it!" he shouted, "You're frightening her."

The crowd started to move, the noise increased, and the mood changed from panic to anger. Lilana squeezed her eyes tightly shut.

Suddenly Vinnie heard a voice he recognised, hollering from the back of the cavern. "Move… I said move! What's all this about? Out of my way!" The mob began to part as Groggles were shoved left and right, until eventually a familiar face appeared in front of them.

"Gelda?!" Vinnie ran towards his friend, "Are we pleased to see you!"

Gelda stepped back, her face warped in anger. "Pleased to see me? Pah!" she spat. "I shouldn't even be here. In fact, I wouldn't be here if it wasn't for you and your big mouth."

Vinnie stepped forward, shocked and confused. "What are you talking about?"

Gelda shook her head, "I'm talking about you telling someone where we were. We asked you specifically not to tell anyone. We trusted you; we helped you!"

Vinnie's eyes dropped. "I only told my parents. They wouldn't have mentioned it, they just wouldn't."

"Well clearly they did. Those Seekers are very persuasive. They came and destroyed our home. Pulled it apart until there was nothing left. Mrs Muddles and I were dragged here and we lost everything. Because of you!" Gelda reached back and pulled on the arm of an unseen Groggle, swinging her forward into the light to face Vinnie.

Lilana peered through her fingers to see Mrs Muddles, crouched, tiny and frail. Her hands were bruised and twisted into knots; her eyes dark and wrinkled. She was broken and sad and Lilana couldn't bare it. She rushed forward and held her. "I'm so sorry," she wept as she squeezed her tightly.

"Sorry!" sneered Gelda. "That's just perfect. All is forgiven in that case!"

She turned to pull Mrs Muddles back into the crowd but felt a tug of resistance. Mrs Muddles looked back and forced a smile. "Lilana my darling, thank you for your apology. I know you didn't mean for this to happen. Please excuse Gelda, she is worried for me." Gelda huffed and Mrs Muddles continued. "This is it for us now. We just need to accept it, you included. My home is gone. I have nothing, will always have nothing and will always be nothing." She paused to rub her eyes before walking away. "They can have half of my food," she announced to everyone and the crowd dispersed.

Lilana watched as they disappeared into the crowd. She felt more alone than she had ever felt. She had never lost a friend before. It tugged on her heart and lurched in her gut. The guilt sat, heavy in her stomach as it rumbled with hunger. She remembered everything that Mrs Muddles had done for them. When bread was thrown at Lilana, she ate it, although every bite reminded her of the sacrifices Mrs Muddles continued to make.

While the Groggles slept, Vinnie and Lilana sat in silence. Unable to speak, they held hands and awaited their fate.

Morning came, and with it the rattle of the gates opening, the gobbling of hungry mouths guzzling down bread, and the scuffle of feet on the dirt as the Groggles left to mine the crystals. Alone, Vinnie and Lilana moved to the front of the cavern and watched as the rock crumbled and crystals toppled down to the ground. They both rubbed their periapts, aware of the suffering endured to make them.

"Why so sad?" Chordata appeared from the passageway carrying Lilana's bag. "You two are about to meet Regent Monelda. You should be feeling privileged, excited even, not sobbing through the bars like a pair of babies."

Vinnie grunted. "I'm not excited to meet a tyrant who would allow this sort of treatment of people!"

"People?" Chordata scoffed, "These are Groggles, not people and they are exactly where they should be. They have a job to do and they are doing it. They should be grateful for the food and shelter."

Vinnie winced at her prejudice. "You really are something else Chordata."

"I know," she smiled smugly as she opened the cage, "I am indeed quite something."

Lilana shook her head.

"You disagree do you Lilana?" Chordata barked as Lilana felt her spine tingle and arms become heavy. "Always just staring at me, with that disapproving look Lilana, and now shaking your head. You always think you are so much better than me, always have; well look at you now."

Lilana's arms had become numb and her legs could not move. She was paralysed.

Chordata crept towards her. Like a venomous spider stalking its prey, she circled her. "Poor little Lilana, always looking on and judging but never actually doing anything about it. Clinging to your little bag of flowers and leaves. Pathetic." She threw the bag into the cavern.

"I mean you judge me, you look down on me, you give me those disgusted looks and now this shake of the head. Is that it? Is that the best you can do? A head shake? Let's be honest about this. You watch all this happen, you disagree with it, yet you sit in the corner and let it happen. You do nothing! In my opinion, if you do nothing, then you are as responsible for all this as me!"

Lilana cringed, tears escaping although she begged them not to.

Chordata spotted them and grinned. "Crying? A head shake and tears is what you're going with. Typical Lilana. Do you think your sister would be stood weeping like a baby? How many times did she try to escape and fail? I don't know, but I do know she never gave up. And your friend Vinnie, always jumping to your side, fearless, brave… Stupid and pathetic, but at least he tries. But you, Lilana, you sit by and let bad things happen while you quiver in fear. You are pathetic and you are spineless. You are a coward!"

Lilana spotted Mrs Muddles lifting rubble into baskets. She had stopped to watch Chordata and a soldier was poking her with a stick. She shoved him and he pushed her to the ground. She glanced up and gave Lilana a smile. In the face of adversity Mrs Muddles found a moment to show Lilana it was ok.

Chordata glimpsed at Vinnie who stood, immobile and unable to speak. Looking back at Lilana she noticed something seemed different. Lilana's eyes were glazed and dark. Her hair was whipping back and forth across her face and her mouth held an expression Chordata had not seen before. Her periapt was illuminated and pulsating.

It started as a low rumble that caused the Groggles to swing back and forth on their ropes. Quickly lowering themselves to the ground, they clung to the rocks as the low rumbling came closer. The ground began to rock back and forth.

Chordata stumbled over to the rock face and clutched at rocks that jutted out until she was stable. "What's happening?!" she shouted to her soldiers. They had tumbled to the ground and were grabbing at the rocks around them.

The ground surrounding Lilana started to crumble away, the soil shifting as if something were drilling its way to the surface. Suddenly, a gigantic, brown, twisted root shot out of the earth, showering Lilana with dusty brown soil. It was closely followed by more roots, one by one, boring up through the earth and bursting out into the cave. Lilana's eyes shot to Chordata and the roots followed, chasing her across the cave and dragging her away from the passage. Throwing her from root to root, they juggled her across the cave, to face Lilana, wrapping around her and squeezing her tight.

More roots came smashing through the walls of the cave, coiling round the soldiers as they

142

trampled along the ground, pinning them to the walls and hanging them from the ceiling. No soldier was spared. The air was filled with clouds of soil as they swung in the dusty breeze.

As the dust settled, Lilana stared at Chordata as the root entwined around her squeezed more tightly. The more she stared, the tighter it squeezed, until Chordata relented. Lilana felt the numbness give way to feeling, as she was able to move her legs. She ran to Vinnie. "Let him go too!" she demanded. Vinnie dropped to the ground.

"Well, Lilana, you really know how to surprise a person," he said as he dusted off his clothes. "Now let's get out of here."

"Everyone needs to get out of here," she answered as she ran towards Mrs Muddles, who hugged her and ruffled her hair. "I knew you could do it, Lilana," she gushed.

They began loading up the Groggles onto the lifting platforms in groups of ten. "When you get up there you need to drop the platform and scatter in pairs to find a safe place to hide," Vinnie instructed as he raised the platforms. "Go as far away as you can."

Groggles piled onto the platforms, thanking Lilana as they passed her. They continued to raise and drop the platforms until the only ones left were Gelda and Mrs Muddles.

Mrs Muddles hugged Lilana, then Vinnie, and held their hands. "You are truly remarkable," she admired. "Find your friend and then come and find us. You are always welcome. Always."

Gelda nodded in agreement, patting them both on the back as she jumped onto the platform to join her friend. "Come and find us," she insisted.

Vinnie raised the platform as Lilana trotted over to Chordata, still wrapped in the tree root. She looked angry and deflated. "I may be quiet, and I may be slow to act, but I know the love of friendship. I would do anything to protect the people I care about," Lilana declared. "You were right about one thing though, not acting when you see something wrong is as bad as doing it yourself. I plan to change that. However, enslaving people because someone tells you to is an act of fear, Chordata, not courage. You are the coward."

Lilana snatched up her bag and ran towards the platform, jumping up as it rose into the ceiling. She watched as the slave mine disappeared into the darkness below.

Chapter 16: Finding a Friend in the Fog

Lilana and Vinnie clambered over the edge of the wooden platform and landed with a crunch onto the frosty grass. Like an icy blanket, every blade in the meadow twinkled with droplets of frozen dew.

They watched as the Groggles bounced into the woods on the horizon; their pink feet padding on logs and branches as they bounded across the foliage and disappeared behind the camouflage of the forest floor.

Vinnie rummaged around amongst the sticks and rubble on the ground. "We need to get those lifts out of action," he ordered, rustling underneath a pile of leaves. "We need something sharp to cut the ropes. Help me, Lilana."

Lilana, in a quiet daze as she watched her friends vanish from view, sprang into action. Scampering around, she searched beneath piles of twigs and leaves for a sharp stone. "Ouch!" she squeaked, pulling her hand back from beneath some grass. Blood trickling down her finger, she popped it into her mouth as she kicked the twigs away to reveal a small, pointed stone.

146

"You ok?" Vinnie rushed over and picked up the blood-tinged stone.

"I'm fine," mumbled Lilana, removing her finger from her mouth. The bleeding had slowed. She rummaged in her bag for some Hittle Moss that she wrapped around it, and held it in place with a small piece of string.

Meanwhile Vinnie set about cutting the ropes, rubbing away at the thick twine with the sharpened tool until, fibre by fibre, they snapped. One by one, the ropes broke until the wooden platforms hung by a single cord, swinging from side to side in the lift shaft. Without warning, they dropped into the abyss below, landing with a crash that echoed through the shaft for several seconds, before withdrawing into an eerie silence.

Vinnie approached Lilana. "Well I don't know where that came from, Lilana, but it was amazing. I mean, you destroyed a mine!"

Lilana smiled. "I guess I decided not to be afraid anymore," she answered, pleased with herself.

"But Lilana the power – I mean, I've seen you natter to Nora Flowers, chat to Elmberries, unravel a few vines… but you commanded a forest, Lilana! A forest!" Vinnie couldn't help but stare at Lilana with awe and admiration.

"It just came over me, Vinnie, like I was being overtaken." She paused to breathe, "It rose up within me and I felt, well, I felt powerful. I knew exactly what to do and how to do it."

"Wow!" exclaimed Vinnie, "I wonder if that will ever happen to me."

"Of course it will!" Lilana assured him before changing the subject. "Sorry Vinnie, we need to get out of here, before they break free."

Looking around, surveying their surroundings, Vinnie felt uncertain. "Where are we Lilana?" Everything looked unfamiliar and familiar all at once, just grass and trees, grass and trees.

Lilana had absolutely no idea either. That well-known feeling of worry crept over her as she started to panic. Spotting Lilana's anxious expression, Vinnie took charge. He flung her bag over his shoulder and grabbed her arm. "Come on Lilana, let's find Kitty and Jasper. They will have headed to the Stronghold by now so we will head there."

Lilana stared blankly into the woods, and then into the meadow as if trying to decide. "This way," instructed Vinnie as he dragged her into the meadow.

Crunching through the frozen grass, they meandered across the fields and away from the forest. Vinnie knew that the Groggles would not be heading anywhere near the Stronghold and had decided to go in the opposite direction.

As the sun rose, the grass thawed and a low mist hovered above the ground, enveloping their feet. They walked, as if floating on a foggy river, wading towards the hazy distance.

Lilana shivered and Vinnie rubbed her arms. It was cold and he was hungry. They needed to find somewhere to shelter and warm up, but there was nowhere in sight.

In the distance, the fog seemed to thicken and puff up from the ground into clouds. Lilana strained to see, confused by the thick column of fog rising from the earth. "What's that?" she asked, pointing up ahead.

"Fog," retorted Vinnie, confused by the question. "The same fog we are trudging through."

149

Lilana shook her head. "It's different Vinnie. Look it's coming up from the ground."

Vinnie stopped to study the meadow ahead and shrugged. "Looks the same to me," he replied, continuing forward. Lilana followed a few steps behind, not convinced.

As they approached, the air thickened with moisture and the column of steam chuffed up into the sky. The air became warm and damp, and Lilana's hair clung to her face.

"It's a hot pool!" proclaimed Vinnie as he ran and vanished into the mist. "Come on, Lilana."

Lilana wafted at the fog as she followed, until she found Vinnie sat on the side of a bubbling pool of crystal-clear water. Unable to see beyond her own feet, she felt uneasy, but the warmth of the pool lured her to its edge. Crossing her legs, she leaned up against him and closed her eyes. It was so good to finally be warm.

"I'm so hungry, Lilana," Vinnie announced. "What can we eat? I've seen nothing nearby and my stomach is starting to hurt."

Raising her head, Lilana rifled in her bag pulling out two jars. She filled them with herbs, berries and a few nuts. Then she dipped them in the pool, immersing them under the water. As they filled, she gave them a stir. "Leave them for an hour or so," she instructed, yawning and leaning again on Vinnie's shoulder.

When she awoke, Vinnie was lifting the jars out of the pool. They had turned a deep brown colour. Their fragrant aroma wafted into Lilana's nostrils; her stomach rumbled in anticipation.

They ate the broth hungrily, dipping small chunks of bread and thrusting them into their mouths. Warm and satisfied, they considered what to do next.

"We just need to keep moving until we find someone who can tell us the way?" suggested Vinnie.

"But what if we are going in completely the wrong direction?" argued Lilana. "We could be heading back to Elmsmere for all you know."

Shuddering at the thought, Vinnie paused. "I don't know what else to suggest Lilana, we don't have a whole lot of options."

Lilana nodded in agreement. "I know," she relented. "I just hoped we might have come up with a better idea."

"Shhh!" hushed Vinnie. "Did you just hear that?"

"What?" whispered Lilana. "What was it?"

Vinnie pointed behind them. "A rustling noise from over there," he mouthed. Lilana looked confused, unable to understand a word.

The fog in front of them wavered, and, breaking through it, a brown furry nose sniffed and snuffled its way towards their faces. Vinnie froze as its owner stepped forward through the misty curtain.

"It's a Pelnack," Lilana smiled as she gave its nose a rub. Its nose continued to sniffle and snuffle, until it reached their empty broth jars, where its long tongue licked them clean. Lilana tickled its ears and it laid beside them. "It must have smelt the food," she laughed.

Vinnie's eyes came to life, an idea forming behind them. Lilana didn't like that look. She'd seen it before.

"That's it!" he cried. "The perfect solution." Lilana looked bewildered as Vinnie announced, "We will ride the Pelnack. We can see everything up there and can go for miles. We will find the Stronghold in no time."

"Firstly, there is no cart," she pointed out. "And secondly... and this may be the biggest sticking point... neither of us can talk to animals."

"Pah," grumbled Vinnie, "I said it then and I'll say it now. Anyone can ride a Pelnack. It doesn't take a gift to hop on its back and give its fur a tug."

Seizing the last of the bread, he lured the Pelnack onto the meadow. Lilana watched on apprehensively.

Once in the meadow, Vinnie crept closer, the bread dangling between his fingers, "Hello, little fella," he muttered, stepping closer. "How'd you like to fly us to the Stronghold?" The Pelnack snorted at the bread, its tongue feeling the air around it. Vinnie stepped closer still, his fingers clasping tight to the bread as the Pelnack caught it with its tongue and began sucking it in.

Close now, Vinnie reached up, grabbed a fistful of fur, and in a flash, he swung himself up

153

and over, landing gently between the Pelnack's hidden wings. "See, no problem," he grinned.

On finishing its snack, the Pelnack felt Vinnie's presence and rose up. It jumped in the air, kicking first its front then its back legs as Vinnie flipped up and down… eventually landing with a plonk on his bottom.

Lilana chuckled at Vinnie, who looked both stunned and excited, as he sat between the Pelnack's legs. This time it nuzzled at him, picking him up by his collar and flinging him back between its wings. As if he was saying, "You are welcome to ride, but I am in charge."

Lilana smirked as Vinnie announced, "See Lilana, easy peasy. You coming?" She climbed up its legs and rested behind Vinnie, holding on tightly to its thick fur. Vinnie ruffled its ears again and gave a nudge with his knees. Its magnificent wings unfolded. Lilana remembered how magnificent they were as they flapped above her, creating wind all of their own. The Pelnack thundered across the meadow, before they were lifted gracefully into the air and swept up into the sky.

Chapter 17: Travelling by Driftle

Kitty had looked everywhere for Vinnie and Lilana, and, as much as she didn't want to believe it, she was beginning to think that Jasper was right. Vinnie and Lilana had gone on without them.

"I just don't understand why they would disappear like that?" she questioned. "Vinnie can be a hot head, but Lilana would have calmed him down." She sat on a log, head in hands, kicking the leaves at her feet in frustration.

Jasper sat next to her, rubbing his injured leg. "Look, maybe they decided to find somewhere to hide out for a bit. Or maybe they decided not to go to the Stronghold after all."

Kitty shook her head. "Lilana would never leave Iris. The whole point of us going there is to get her."

Jasper nodded. "That's true, but they have gone. We don't know where, but we can't sit and wait for them forever."

Kitty knew that Jasper was right. They couldn't wait forever, but surely they could wait for a little longer. "Look Jasper, they wanted to wait until morning to leave. Maybe this is their way of making us do that. Let's wait until morning. If they don't arrive we will head out."

Jasper nodded in agreement. "Ok, let's do that, " he winced as he peeled back the Hittle Moss on his wound. "It's definitely looking better. By morning it might have healed."

When morning came, Vinnie and Lilana were still nowhere to be seen. Kitty sat drinking her Elmberry tea, searching the woods for them, longing for them to appear. How could they do this to her? Why would they do this to her?

"Morning Kitty," Jasper strolled into the clearing smiling. His leg, it seemed, was healed. "That Hittle Moss is fantastic stuff!" he exclaimed. "Your friend Lilana's quite the healer."

Kitty sighed. "They haven't returned then?" she asked, knowing full well the answer was no.

Jasper joined her on the log. "They will catch up with us Kitty," he reassured. "We can't wait around for them – we will be spotted sooner or later. And imagine how pleased Lilana will be if we bring Iris back. We will come back here as soon as we get her. That is if they don't catch up with us."

"Fine," Kitty muttered as she stood, swept her hair back, and started off across the plain, Jasper trotting behind to catch up.

As they walked, the cool breeze and fresh smell of the woods lifted Kitty's spirits. Striding through the grass, watching the Pelnacks nibbling at their breakfast, she felt calm and positive about the future.

"What do you think it's like, this Hidden Haven?" she asked, turning to Jasper.

"I don't know," he answered. "I guess it's guarded, somewhere secluded, and away from the reach of Seekers."

"I hope it's full of plants for Lilana to tend," she pondered. "Do you think Vinnie's family could come and stay? I bet they could. And Iris could be a look out. I just want us all to be together and happy. I want us all to be happy." Her smile drooped into a frown, her thoughts returning to Lilana and Vinnie. They had never let each other down. Vinnie gave up his family for them. Why would they just disappear? Was she too hard on Vinnie? Had she driven him away?

She turned to Jasper who was pulling handfuls of grass and throwing them into the air. "Do you think I was too hard on him, Jasper?"

Jasper stopped and took her by the shoulders. "Kitty, you have been nothing but a good friend. If they can't see that, then they don't deserve you. If I'm being honest, I think they've gone off for a grump. Vinnie has left his family. Lilana misses hers. You are their friend, Kitty, but family – well, family is different."

Kitty's shoulders dropped, reminded again that she had no family and, in fact, had little or no knowledge about who she was. "I'm just glad that I have you Jasper," she uttered.

Jasper tapped her on the head playfully. "We don't need family, Kitty, we have everything we need right here. Besides, at some point they will stop having a grumble and catch us up. Lilana wants to find Iris. They are not far behind I'm sure. Now come and look at this!" He raced off into the grass and Kitty rushed after him.

The grass was tall and Kitty had to sweep it aside to push through. Hot on Jasper's heels, she galloped through the field. Just in front she saw

Jasper, crouched on the ground, peering through the grass. She skidded to a halt, slamming into him with a thump. "Sorry," she giggled.

"Look!" he hissed. "Look through here."

Kitty peered through the grass. Grazing in a small meadow, she could see three of the hairiest creatures that she had ever seen in her life. About two metres tall, with big brown eyes and long black eyelashes that fluttered in the breeze, the animals were truly majestic. Their bodies were covered in thick, soft hair that flowed down to the ground and wafted back and forth in the breeze. "They are incredible!" Kitty exclaimed in amazement. "Are they floating?"

Vinnie chuckled. "No the hair is so long it covers their legs. Beautiful, aren't they?"

Kitty nodded as she admired the long white horns protruding from their heads, twisting up and around into the perfect spiral. "Can you talk to them?" she asked.

"I hope so," he replied. These guys are our ticket into the Stronghold. Kitty looked confused.

As Jasper pointed up onto the hill, Kitty could see herds of the beasts grazing into the horizon. "The Stronghold is beyond that hill. We will be spotted as soon as we leave the coverage of the plains. We need to hitch a ride. My friends the Driftles will make the perfect steeds."

Still confused, Kitty took a second look. "I don't get it. Surely riding on the back of an enormous, white, hairy beast is pretty conspicuous?"

"Who said anything about riding on their backs?" Jasper grinned.

Tiptoeing onto the meadow and careful not to scare them off, he began purring and humming, to get their attention. Taking no notice, they tore mouthfuls of the tall grass from above him. Green dribble oozed from between their teeth and dripped from their white beards, landing on his forehead and trickling down his cheek. Kitty muffled her sniggers and she urged him to try again.

Stepping closer, his purrs were louder this time and the Driftles seemed to sway along to the low hum of Jasper's song. They began to move towards him. Kitty saw a flash of fear in Jasper's eyes and she swallowed. The first to reach him was the largest. It began nodding its head and purring

160

back. Jasper reached out to rub its wet, pink nose. It stepped forward and nudged him, knocking him to the ground.

Clambering to his feet, Jasper reached out again. The Driftle gently nuzzled his hand this time. Their conversation continued. Eventually Jasper gestured for Kitty to join him.

Kitty limped over, hiding behind her dark hair for fear of showing them exactly how afraid she was. Kitty Midnight was never afraid. Reaching out tentatively, she touched a leg. The hair was softer than anything she had ever touched; she ran her fingers through it over and over again.

"Watch me and do the same as I do," Jasper instructed as he parted the Driftles hair and disappeared inside. After a few minutes, a hand appeared through the fur and Kitty stepped closer to take a peek.

Jasper lay under the belly of the Driftle, supported by a hair hammock he had fashioned by looping clumps of the long hair underneath him. Hidden by the flowing locks of the Driftle, Jasper was invisible. "Warm, cosy and invisible. What more could you ask for?" he announced with a grin.

Kitty approached the nearest Driftle, ruffling its hair. "Hello there, big fella. I hope this is all ok with you?" Turning its head, it nudged her towards the hairy curtain. She parted it and stepped inside. Looping chunks of hair and tying them to support her, she grabbed onto the legs and shimmied up. Finally, leaning back and resting into the hammock, she sighed with a satisfied grin. Popping her hand through the curtain, she gave Jasper a thumbs up. The Driftle rumbled into action as they began their silent climb to the Stronghold.

Chapter 18: Turning the Tables

Kitty had slept comfortably for most of the journey, nestled by the soft fur and warm belly of the Driftle and soothed by its purring lullaby. Jasper's Driftle was less of a purrer and more of a grunter. Startled by loud snorts and intermittent galloping, Jasper had lain awake, clinging to the Driftle legs while it thundered back and forth across the fields. As for the loud and drooly chewing, he heard every munch, crunch, lick, dribble and swallow.

Climbing out of her hammock, Kitty skirted out onto the fresh grass and stretched her arms up into the sky. Jasper was rubbing his eyes and grumbling as he twisted his back and flinched. "Worst journey of my life," he moaned, "That thing didn't stop eating. And when it wasn't gobbling down every leaf in sight, it was racing back and forth, back and forth. Stupid animal."

Kitty yawned. "Come on Jasper, he got you here, you should be grateful."

"Sorry, you're right," Jasper replied. "I'm just tired."

"Where are we anyway?" asked Kitty, looking around. All she could see was tall grass and white fur.

Jasper parted the grass to reveal a gravel pathway. Riddled with weeds and twigs, it led up to an old red door with peeling paint and a dull brass handle covered in notches.

"That has not exactly answered my question," stated Kitty as she rolled her eyes.

Jasper raised his eyebrows. "Look up," he instructed.

Kitty gasped as her eyes flitted from the doorway to the air floating above them. Towering into the sky, climbed a red stone tower that grazed the clouds with its black slate roof. One of six columns, it was joined to the others by a red stone wall: smooth and impenetrable. Tall grass climbed the fortress, tickling the stone as it brushed against it.

"The Stronghold," she declared. "How do we get in? Surely a doorway is just… too simple."

"In Melgron Barracks we were taught about the Stronghold. This is the soldiers' entrance," Jasper explained as he approached the doorway.

164

"What are you doing?" whispered Kitty, reaching to grab him. "You'll be seen! What's the plan, just stroll up and hope we blend in. We'll be spotted straight away."

Jasper gave a knowing smile. "Behind this door is a storeroom: uniforms, weapons... that sort of thing. We will dress like soldiers and, as you said, blend in."

Kitty nodded. "Ok," she agreed. "How are you planning to open it?"

Jasper stepped closer and jiggled the handle. "It's locked," he declared. Kitty rolled her eyes again.

Scuttling back, Jasper shrugged. "Let's just wait in the grass until someone comes," he suggested.

"Then what?" asked Kitty, beginning to get irritated by the haphazard attempt at a plan.

"Shhh," muttered Jasper, pushing her back into the grass.

Approaching along the path were two soldiers. Towering above the children and dressed head to toe in scarlet, they mimicked the Stronghold they were here to protect. Their uniforms were trimmed with black buttons. Perched on top of their heads were small, square, black hats.

Silently, they proceeded to the door. On arrival, the smaller solider pulled on a crystal-shaped button on his jacket. It came free. He pressed it into one of the notches on the handle, turned it clockwise and the door opened. Kitty watched as the soldiers disappeared inside and the door gently closed. But, before it could shut completely, Jasper streaked into view. He placed a small rock at the base of the door and scuttled back into the grass. The door was open a crack. A slither of light glistening through the slit.

They waited several minutes to be sure the soldiers had gone, then, creeping up to the doorway, they sneaked inside and closed the door.

Closing her eyes, Kitty willed her breathing to slow and her heart to stop pounding. Jasper was calmly rummaging through the uniforms hanging from wooden pegs along the wall. "Come on, Kitty, stop gasping for air like a fish and grab some boots."

Kitty dropped to her knees and crawled amongst the boots lined up neatly under the wooden benches. The stench of damp feet drifted into her nostrils and she started to wretch. Grasping a pair that looked small enough, she stood up and let out a deep breath. "You can do this," she whispered.

Jasper bundled a uniform into her arms. "Get dressed," he ordered.

Marching along the halls of the Stronghold, Kitty felt her hands shake. "Let's just get Iris and get out of here," she whispered nervously to Jasper who was pacing in front.

"There is a lookout balcony at the front of the fortress wall," Jasper replied, "We will start there." He turned into a small opening on the right and began climbing a narrow stairwell.

The top of the stairs opened out into a hallway. Jasper continued marching along as it widened into what seemed to be a meeting room. Furnished with an oval, black marble table and surrounded by large, wooden, red chairs carved into the shapes of birds, its grandeur seemed a little much for a lookout. Kitty spotted the balcony up ahead, but it was empty. "She's not here," she whispered.

Jasper didn't respond. "Jasper, Jasper!" her voice cracking into a low screech. "She isn't there." Jasper turned a corner and Kitty followed.

"This took longer than expected, Jasper," a voice bellowed from behind a long, purple, velvet curtain, neatly trimmed with gold fringe and scarlet beads.

"I'm sorry," he replied. "There were a few… incidents."

"Hmm," the voice scoffed.

Confused, Kitty watched as two soldiers appeared to pull back the velvet curtain. Jasper stepped backwards to stand in line with them, as a woman stepped out onto the green marble floor.

She emerged from behind the curtain, her green eyes flashing Kitty an angry glare. Her face contorted with rage, she stepped closer. "Show me your wrist," she demanded.

Kitty looked to Jasper, who stared straight through her. What was happening? What was he doing? She raised her arm to reveal her periapt.

Dull and blackened, the cat looked sad and defeated.

"What's this, Jasper?" the woman screeched, Kitty's arm flailing around in the air.

Jasper stepped forward. "It's her, my Regent. She told me her story." He said shuffling back.

Her smooth, blonde hair tumbled down her back like rippling silk as she turned towards Jasper. Kitty's boots scuffed along the marble as she was dragged along and thrown at his feet. Her wrist, still clasped by the Regent, was thrust into his face. "This, Jasper, is not a green crystal."

Jasper admired the crystal for a few seconds and then rubbed it with his thumb. The dull black of the crystal began to change colour, slowly brightening, until a glint of green caught the light, throwing an emerald flash across the room.

Regent Monelda dropped Kitty's arm. "Get up!" she demanded, "Where is Heragus. I need him. Someone find him now." A soldier scarpered off into the hallway.

"So, you are the one who killed my sweet Emmeline," the Regent snarled as her green eyes met Kitty's.

Kitty looked to Jasper and then back at Monelda. It was a mistake. It was definitely a mistake. They had the wrong person. Flooded with relief, her fear washed away. She spoke confidently. "You have the wrong person, I've never killed anybody in my life. I'm a little sharp at times, but kill someone? No, that's not me."

Monelda paced the room. Agitated and upset she talked, as if to herself. "My sweet Emmeline. She was the perfect sister. She was the only person who loved me, who understood me, who knew how I felt. She would give anything to anyone. Anything."

Kitty pleaded. "I have never met your sister, let alone hurt her. I've been in the Academy all my life. I'm so sorry you lost her, but it wasn't me."

Monelda turned, her eyes wild and her face red with rage. She stormed towards Kitty. "She would give anything for anyone; anything! And she gave her life to give you yours, Kitty Midnight!"

Her words hovered in the air, buzzing in Kitty's ear as Monelda flew towards her. Kitty threw her arms over her head.

"STOP MONELDA!" the voice boomed. "She is a child. She is your sister's child. Emmeline would not want this."

Peering through her arms, Kitty watched as a dark-haired man in a black uniform swooped in and wrapped Monelda in his black-feathered cloak.

Kitty's head was swimming. Unable to take it all in she dropped to her knees.

The Regent, calmer now, addressed Jasper. "Well done, Jasper. You have proved your loyalty and your worth. You will be rewarded. Take this murderer to the cells."

"As for you," she added, turning her attention to Kitty. "You are lucky, Kitty Midnight. Today is not your day to die, and you have Heragus to thank for that. But I will think of a suitable punishment for you, something torturous and unbearable like the life I've had to lead without my beloved sister."

Jasper stepped forward. "My Regent, there is something else," he barked. "She wasn't alone.

She had two friends with her: a boy and a girl. The girl was the sister of one of your lookouts, Iris. They were heading here to find her."

"Take her to the cells. Then find this Iris and bring her to me," ordered Monelda.

Jasper grabbed Kitty's arm and she prized it off. "Get off me!" she snapped, "I don't need you to touch me, I can walk by myself."

Heragus escorted Monelda to her throne as Kitty was led away.

Chapter 19: The Ratlings

"How could you do this to me?" Kitty muttered as they tramped down the spiral staircase into the depths of the Stronghold. As they meandered down into the pit, the air became cooler and damp. Kitty shivered. "I thought we were friends."

"That is exactly your problem, Kitty." Jasper stopped at the bottom of the steps. "You think that you need friends, that you need family, that you need someone... just anyone. It's time you realised that many of us were dumped by our families; hated and despised by the people around us. They are disgusted by us and afraid of us. Your friends abandoned you for goodness sake. Your best friends. Don't you get it? The only person in the world that you need is yourself. Monelda trains us, feeds us, and gives us a home. If we are loyal, she shows us gratitude. I don't need anything else."

"I don't believe that you have no feelings, Jasper. We shared time together and we bonded. We ARE friends," Kitty held his arm. "You are not a monster, Jasper."

Jasper held her hand and smiled. "I am not a monster, Kitty. I am also not your friend. I pretended to be your friend to get you here. I preyed on your insecurities to my advantage. I mean, did you not wonder why the Stronghold was so quiet? Did you not think it strange that I knew how to get here so easily? How I knew my way round? Blinded by friendship, your stupidity landed you here, Kitty Midnight."

Kitty dropped her arm as he pushed her forward into a dark corridor. Shoving her into the nearest open cell, the gate clanged shut behind her.

Jasper pressed his face against the bars and smirked. "The Seekers took me from my home when I was six. My parents begged them to let me stay here. I have two sisters who are both soldiers here at the Stronghold. How cruel it seems that I have a family that I don't care for; and you are desperate for a family that you will never have." Jasper tapped the bars in a chirpy rhythm and strolled away into the darkness.

The cell was windowless and lit only by a small candle in the corner of the room. It rested on a wooden box next to a pile of blankets that reminded her of the Slump in the Groggles burrow. She bundled herself into it. Tough and prickly, they scratched her face as she wept into them. Finally, she had a piece of the puzzle she had always wanted; an understanding of where she came from and who she was. But with that knowledge came disappointment and grief. She wept for the loss of the mother she had never known.

Hearing footsteps on the stairs, she huddled into the corner. Sneaking a look through the blankets, she spotted a plate being slid underneath the gate. It skidded to a halt in the centre of the room. Waiting for the footsteps to leave, she collected the plate and devoured its stale contents. She closed her eyes and sniffed as she remembered the smell of Raina's Bungle pie baking in the oven. How she would love a taste of that now.

Her thoughts turned to Vinnie and Lilana. They had abandoned her in the woods. They had left her because they didn't need her; because she didn't have a gift, no doubt. What use was she to them? It was all coming together now. The more she thought about it the more it made sense. When she was strong, they wanted her; but weakened by their friendship and her longing for acceptance, they no longer needed her.

Maybe Jasper was right? When she was at Elmsmere she didn't have anyone and she was fine. And look what friendship and family had done to her. She kicked the plate across the room. It bounced off the wall with a clank that echoed through the hallway.

She would never trust anyone again. She had started life alone and she would stay that way.

....

Monelda paced, her hair trailing behind her, while Heragus sat at the table watching as she drifted from wall to wall. "I will just leave her there to rot. That's what I'll do," she declared. "I can't look at her. Just knowing she is alive is rattling enough."

"Would Emmeline want that?" Heragus asked, lifting himself from his seat. "She is your niece and Emmeline loved her."

Monelda span round. "Emmeline loved me, Heragus! Me! She didn't love that little Ratling. She never even met her."

"Of course, my Regent," Heragus bowed, "But you cannot leave your own flesh and blood to rot in a cell."

Monelda pondered the thought. A smile crept onto her face. "She can work in the yard with the other little Ratlings. That's it! I will never see her down there."

"As you wish, my Regent," Heragus agreed.

As he spoke, Jasper marched in, followed by a girl with blue eyes so bright that the room seemed to light up before her. They sparkled as she walked, twinkling with each step. Like all Monelda's soldiers, her brown hair was tied tightly in a bun.

"You are Iris?" asked Heragus. Iris nodded.

"Jasper has found Kitty Midnight, my sister's child," Monelda spat the words as if their sourness offended her tongue. "He tells me that your sister was with her and was planning to take you from here. Did you know about this?"

Iris didn't look up from the ground as she answered. "Of course not, my Regent. I am grateful for what I have here. If she was coming, she decided this alone. On reaching here, she would have been disappointed, as this is my home. I have no intention of leaving."

Satisfied with her answer, Monelda nodded. "And rightly so," she agreed.

"They will not be coming," Jasper spoke again. "The sister and her friend left us in the woods and, we assume, went back to his family. They were fearful of you, my Regent."

Monelda addressed Iris. "You may go back to your post and have extra bread at dinner," she instructed. Iris scampered across the room, disappearing round the corner.

"Jasper, take Kitty to the yard," Monelda commanded. "She will live among the Ratlings."

Jasper bowed his head, "Yes, my Regent."

....

Kitty awoke to hear the gate rattle and clunk. Jumping to her feet she saw Jasper standing in the entrance. "It's your lucky day!" he announced. "Monelda has granted you mercy, well sort of. You are going to work in the yard, with your own kind."

Kitty grunted. "As long as I don't have to look at your face again, it sounds perfect."

178

Jasper gasped mockingly. "Oh I'm wounded Kitty, that really has damaged our friendship."

"I don't have friends," she barked as she followed him out.

The yard was a large, stone courtyard in the centre of the Stronghold. Teaming with small, scruffy children, it was split into lots of areas where children were carrying out an array of different tasks.

"These are the Ratlings," smirked Jasper. "A Ratling is a gifted child with a gift so pathetic that Monelda doesn't deem them fit for anything more than cleaning boots or scrubbing clothes. Told you you'd fit right in."

Kitty glared at him. "Get lost, Jasper," she grunted as she ambled across the yard. He disappeared through the nearest exit.

Heavily guarded, the yard was clearly a working prison. Soldiers barked orders at the Ratlings as they rushed about their business: scrubbing plates, kneading bread, washing uniforms. They looked tired and drawn.

Kitty approached a small girl with brown hair with what she initially thought were freckles. On closer inspection, she noticed they were specks of dirt from the boots she was scrubbing. "Do I just pick a job or am I allocated one?" she asked. The girl looked flustered, shook her head and scampered away. "Great," Kitty grumbled, "Just great." She picked up a dirty boot and a brush and started to scrub away at the loose mud.

Chapter 20: Iris see's all

Iris saw them coming and her heart swelled. She had watched them in the far distance and was unsure at first about their intentions. But now they were closer, she was sure. Her little sister had found her and was coming to get her. Lilana had always been quite meek, quietly tending to her plants, ignoring the world around her. She hadn't seen Elmsmere for what it was; she was afraid of what was beyond the wall. Iris had certainly never expected her to escape.

They had all heard the rumours of the escapees, but, when Kitty arrived alone and Jasper had said the others had abandoned the journey, Iris had lost hope. She had never fitted in here; not cruel enough, not heartless enough.

No one had ever escaped from an academy and been successful. Monelda was desperate to find them. No one understood why she was so distressed about Kitty's escape, but now, well now it all made sense.

He had called Iris before Monelda to gloat about his capture of Kitty. He had told Monelda that they were searching for Iris. Monelda wanted to know Iris's involvement. She denied all knowledge of course and Monelda believed her, although Iris had noticed more eyes on her of late.

Jasper was full of spite, vicious with his words and venomous with his actions. After the meeting Jasper approached her, said he had a message for her. Foolishly Iris responded. Jasper taunted, "Lilana said to tell you that she would come and get you, but it's Bungle Berry season and you know how she is with plants." Iris turned and walked away as he chuckled and sniggered.

Yet now she could see them, soaring through the air on some sort of winged beast and landing in a clearing. They were heading for the Stronghold. She had to intercept them.

Iris could only leave her balcony for food, sleep and the toilet. A soldier stood guard by the balcony, ready to pass on any sightings of importance. Iris sidled up to him and tapped his shoulder. "I'm sorry, I really need... well you know... the toilet," she lied, crossing her legs and clasping her stomach.

"Well go on then," he barked. "Hurry up."

Iris tiptoed off into the direction of the nearest bathroom. Then, looking back to check she wasn't being followed, she scarpered into the kitchen and out through the back into the grass of the meadow.

Crashing through the grass, she ran faster than she ever thought she could; the wet grass slapping her cheeks as she crushed it underfoot. She had to get to Lilana before she headed to the Stronghold. As she smashed through the grass, she spotted Lilana in a clearing. Reaching out for her, she felt herself stumble as an invisible force seemed to grab her waist and throw her to the ground.

Lilana looked aghast. "Vinnie, that's Iris!" she yelped, as Iris's assailant suddenly appeared, wrapped around her waist. Unwinding himself, he jumped up, offering her a hand.

"I'm so sorry, Iris. We thought we were under attack," he apologised. "It's, err, great to finally meet you."

Lilana bounded towards Iris, tangling her up in her arms in a desperate embrace. "I've found you," she sniffled. "I've found you."

183

Aware of her limited time, Iris pulled away from Lilana and turned to the Stronghold. "I have to go back," she whispered. "There isn't much time to explain."

"No!" screeched a horrified Lilana, "I've come for you."

"They have Kitty," rushed Iris. "She's the daughter of Monelda's dead sister and they have imprisoned her."

"What?!" Vinnie blurted, looking confused. "Are you sure? Kitty Midnight? Our Kitty?"

Irritated, Iris answered. "Look it's been all over the Stronghold: the news of your escape. Monelda was furious that you'd managed it, but she was even more anxious to get Kitty back, really anxious."

"What about Jasper?" Lilana asked, fearful for her new friend.

"Jasper?" Iris looked confused, "Jasper is one of Monelda's henchman, he brought Kitty back."

"I knew it!" yelled Vinnie, unable to hide his delight at this revelation.

"Look, it's a long story, but you need to get her out of there. The only way you can do it is with someone on the inside." Iris pointed to the Stronghold, "I'm going back. Just beyond that wall is a yard. Kitty and I will be there in one hour. You need to fly the beast in and get us out."

Iris waved goodbye and Lilana grabbed her hand. "What if I don't see you again? I have missed you so much."

Iris shook her head. "You are Lilana Flowerdew. You've escaped from the Academy, Lilana. You're flying on a Pelnack. There is no way that you won't find your way to me." Pulling her close, she kissed her sister's head. The vines wrapped themselves around Iris, pulling her closer.

"Go," Lilana ordered. "Go!"

Bounding through the grass, Iris raced to get back to her lookout. Whizzing through the kitchen, she dried her face with a cloth and slowed herself back to walking pace as she entered the balcony.

"Where have you been?" questioned the soldier, looking her up and down.

She clutched her stomach. "Lunch didn't agree with me," she answered. "I might have to run off again in a minute."

"Lovely," remarked the soldier, "That's plenty of information, thank you."

Iris, using the sight, stared out into the direction of the yard. Kitty was scrubbing boots. Inseparable from the other poor Ratlings, she looked deflated. Iris had to find a way to get out there.

She was running out of time. If she left her post for a prolonged period, it would rouse suspicion. She was already being watched. There was only one way. It was risky, but Lilana had risked everything to find her, so she had to take the chance.

"Soldier, I need to speak to the Regent. Immediately," she announced.

Chapter 21: The Ratling Rescue

Monelda watched Kitty as she scrubbed, twitching with every movement. Monelda shuddered in disgust. "I can't have her here, Heragus, she is a distraction. You need to dispose of her."

"Stop watching her, my Regent," Heragus suggested as he rolled a map onto the table. "She is not worthy of your focus. Let's concentrate on the task at hand, finding the hide-out the Ratlings speak of."

"Ratlings, pah!" Monelda traced her finger along the map, "They will not hide from me. These children belong to me. I treat them well, feed them, clothe them; then they plot against me, the ungrateful little wretches."

"We will find them and their leader." Heragus nodded in agreement.

Iris entered Monelda's throne room with her head down, afraid her eyes would give away her intentions. Heragus stood tall at the Regent's side. She felt his dark eyes boring into her, searching for the truth.

"Well," asked Monelda impatiently, "What is it?"

Iris, raising her head slightly, gave her answer. "I was looking into the yard today and there were some goings on that seemed suspicious. Some of the children were whispering and passing things amongst themselves." Playing on Monelda's paranoia she explained further. "One of them had a note, my Regent. It said, 'They are coming to take us to ' I thought you would want to know.''

Monelda slammed her fists onto the marble table. It shook as she pounded it again and again. "Who? Who was it? I want to know names, ungrateful Ratlings."

"I'm sorry, my Regent. I only know faces. I can see them from afar, but I can't hear them," Iris stuttered. She was losing her trust, she could feel it.

Heragus stepped forward and the air in the room became still. The breeze seemed to immediately stop flowing. Breathless, Iris gazed up at him. All in black, with eyes to match, he struck fear in all that looked upon him. His feathered cloak hung loosely at his sides. His black periapt caught the light and flickered. "I will take her down to the yard," he thundered as he motioned her to follow. "She can point out the offenders."

Monelda waved her hand in agreement. Iris followed Heragus through the Stronghold and into the yard.

Unprepared for the smell, Iris held her nose and gasped. "Wow, it stinks down here," she muttered. "Phew, yuk!" Heragus forged on. Iris pinched the end of her nose as she followed him into the crowd.

Heragus beckoned her forward. "Can you see the culprits?"

"Well now, let me see." She reviewed the area. "Can we try over there?" Heragus steered her across the yard, taking note as he passed Kitty, scrubbing away at some muddy boots.

"Ok, well, erm, it could have been her?" Iris gestured towards a tall girl with long legs. "Or maybe her," pointing to a stout girl with scruffy, black hair. Heragus shook his head in frustration and strode towards them.

Iris skirted backwards and shuffled towards Kitty. "Kitty? Kitty Midnight?" she asked.

"Do I know you?" Kitty queried, "Because I don't think I do. To be honest, I'm not really into people at the moment." She turned back to scrubbing boots.

"I'm Iris. Your friend, Lilana's sister, Iris?"

"Sorry Iris, I don't have a friend called Lilana," muttered Kitty, throwing the boots down before wandering into the crowd.

Iris grabbed her shoulder. "Kitty, we don't have time for this. They are coming for you. Vinnie and Lilana are coming for you and soon. You need to be ready."

Kitty nudged backwards as Heragus loomed up in front of them, his wide shadow surrounded them, edged with soldiers. "This looks like an interesting meeting," he mused, plucking Iris from the ground, and raising her up above his head.

"Put her down!" demanded Kitty, "She was just checking if I was ok. She hasn't done anything wrong."

Heragus dropped Iris and she plummeted down, landing with a thud, as he turned to address Kitty. "You do not address me. You do not have the right to talk to me. You are a nothing, a no one. If it wasn't for my mercy, you would not be here at all."

Kitty looked around her. The Ratlings had stopped moving. With three hundred eyes waiting for Kitty's response, she took a deep breath. "I am Kitty Midnight, daughter of Regent Emmeline. I will talk to whom ever I choose."

Stunned into silence, no one moved. Heragus leaned in and seized Kitty's arm, hoisting her in into the air and waving her at the crowd like a ragdoll. She flipped and wobbled as he swung her amongst the Ratlings. "It doesn't matter who you are, or who you think you are. You do not address me as an equal unless I decide you are one." Drawing her down to his eye line, his heavy breath in her face he whispered, "You will never be my equal, Kitty Midnight." Then dropped her like a stone.

"Throw them in the cells," he ordered as he stormed back into the Stronghold.

It started as a breeze that tickled their noses and ruffled their hair. As it got stronger, the breeze tugged at their clothes, whipping around them, swirling the dust into cloudy spirals. Children started to cough as the dust rushed into their mouths, clogging their airways. Panic set in as the Ratlings began to scatter in all directions, screaming and shouting for friends and siblings.

Kitty and Iris lay huddled together on the ground. "I think they're here," Kitty declared as she pulled Iris to her feet. Looking up they saw the throbbing wings of a Pelnack, hovering above them, whipping up the air below so that Kitty's black hair twisted and twirled above her. The Pelnack began to descend as the dust cleared, and landed into the middle of the yard.

"Took your time, didn't you," joked Kitty as Lilana slid down the Pelnack's leg and scurried over, grabbing Kitty and Iris all at once, not knowing who to hug first.

Vinnie dangled over the Pelnacks ear. "Told you anyone could drive one of these things," he yelled smugly. Kitty rolled her eyes and smiled.

Footsteps approached and a sense of urgency kicked in. "Come on, let's go!" shouted Kitty, clawing her way up the furry leg, followed by Iris, who was scrambling up behind her.

Already mounted, Lilana held out her hand to swing Kitty up onto its back. "You've changed!" gasped an amazed Kitty, surprised that Lilana had scaled it so quickly. "You have no idea!" replied Lilana beaming.

"Hold tight!" bellowed Vinnie as he ruffled the Pelnack's hair and clenched his knees together. Its wings unfolded and they lifted up into the air, wind rushing around them as they took flight.

Turning to head to the grassy plains, the Pelnack hurtled into the distance.

Relieved, Lilana snuggled into the Pelnack's fur. "Good girl," she muttered, "Good girl." Vinnie looked on as he steered them away from the danger below.

Kitty and Iris shared silent looks. Their eyes met and they nodded. "We need to go back," announced Kitty. "We can't leave them there."

"Who?" questioned Vinnie, "You've got to be kidding me. We only just made it out."

"We made it out once and we can make it out again." Iris gestured to Kitty. "She's right we cannot leave the Ratlings."

"The… what?!" Vinnie snorted. "You want us to risk our lives for... What did you say... Ratlings?"

"They are children," Kitty explained. "Children like us, gifted and good. Monelda doesn't think they are good enough for her needs so she imprisons them. This isn't just about us anymore, don't you see. It's about all of us." Vinnie huffed and dropped his chin into his hands.

Iris nodded in agreement. "What happened to me and what you escaped from – it's happening to children every day. This isn't about escaping from Elmsmere or finding a place to call home. This is about righting a wrong."

Lilana looked back to the Stronghold. "The yard is flooded with soldiers," she observed. "Monelda is furious."

"It's not safe," Vinnie barked. "We go back and it's over for us." He rubbed his eyes. Conflicted, he pondered the safety of his friends. Everything he had fought for was being risked for the lives of these Ratlings; these children! Children like him.

"If we don't go back it's over for them," replied Kitty, pleading with her eyes, knowing deep down that Vinnie's conscience would win out.

"Fine," moaned Vinnie, knowing the route he was about to take was the right one. "Here we go again. Hold on."

Chapter 22: Is it all Over?

Staring up at the sky, Heragus watched as the smudge on the horizon, originally getting smaller, seemed to be increasing in size. Were they coming back?

The soldiers were ushering the children back into the yard, prodding them with sticks and bawling order after order. "Get back to your stations, Ratlings. Those uniforms are not self-cleaning. I said scrub the boots, not tickle them! That bread looks flat – deal with it!"

"Soldiers!" Heragus screamed. "They're coming back. Get ready. I don't care about the rest, but we need Kitty Midnight alive." The soldiers filed into the yard, staring up at brown blur coming into focus quickly.

The Ratlings followed, scattering around the soldiers they looked up as the Pelnack plunged down towards them, bowling the soldiers into the air. They tossed and flipped and landed with thuds. A fine white powder rained down onto them from the dust cloud above and they began to snore.

"Hold your noses!" came a scream from above. "Don't breathe it in. Head for the walls!" The

Ratlings pinched their noses and held their breath as they scarpered towards the fortress walls.

Circling the yard, the Pelnack dropped, depositing an invisible Vinnie into the fray. Dodging between soldiers, he tripped them with his legs, blowing the white dust into their faces as he passed. Soldiers crumbled in his wake; their snores reverberating against the fortress walls.

The Pelnack continued to ground the soldiers, swooping in and out, while Kitty and Lilana sprinkled the Snorosa pollen as they swished by.

The Ratlings started to join the fight, throwing boots at the soldiers who were trying to force them inside. Vinnie continued to sprint from wall to wall. Soldiers collapsed around him as he kicked at their ankles and dosed them with the pollen.

The soldiers' numbers were dwindling; piles of them snoring heaped in every corner, drooling onto their uniforms as they dozed.

The Pelnack dipped down and Vinnie clambered on.

"How are we going to get the children out?" asked Iris as she watched them waving and shouting from below. Desperation in their eyes, they were trapped and there was no way the Pelnack could carry them all.

"I can help with that," Lilana answered as she turned to face the red wall. Her eyes glazed over and she disappeared within herself.

The ground began to shake below them. The long grass started to sink down into the earth. Emerging beside the wall, long, thin roots crept along the ground and wriggled across the red stone. A few swiftly became many. They began slinking between the cracks in the stone, pulling at them and widening them. The cracks started to zig zag down the walls like lightening, shooting from top to bottom and side to side. Tiny at first, they opened up like fresh wounds. The wall began to crumble and flake, stones dropping to the ground, pounding the earth like a thundering rainstorm.

Kitty looked on in amazement as the impenetrable wall smashed to the ground defeated.

Like tiny ants, the Ratlings scuttled over the debris, making a break for freedom. Bolting out into grass, the children ran towards the forest, the sound of the gentle snores of the soldiers fading.

"Time to go," declared Vinnie as the Pelnack beat its wings to prepare to fly.

Monelda trembled with rage as she watched the Ratlings escape over her demolished fortress. "Heragus!!" she screamed, "How has this happened? Get her now! Now!"

Heragus raised his arms and closed his eyes. His feathered cloak fluttered and flapped around him, drifting up to meet his arms. The cloak began to beat against him, flapping along to the rhythm of his heartbeat. His arms joined in, thrusting back and forth as his feet lifted slowly from the ground. He rose up into the air. Spotting the Pelnack flying off towards the forest, he flicked his cloak and soared off towards them.

Kitty held fast to the Pelnack's fur as it glided through the clouds. "Lilana, that was incredible," she congratulated. "I had no idea you could do that."

Lilana blushed as Iris hugged her. "Amazing sister, just amazing."

Vinnie was stroking the ears of the Pelnack as it climbed upwards into the clouds. "Don't worry about thanking me," he grumbled. "I mean, I flew a

199

haired beast, battled some soldiers... A thank you wouldn't... Kitty watch out!!!" He turned to see a huge, black, winged bird swoop in towards Kitty.

"Heragus!" she shouted in surprise as he grabbed her waist and lifted her up into the clouds. Looking down she watched as the Pelnack fell beneath her.

"Kitty!" screamed Lilana. "Vinnie, do something!"

Vinnie held back the urge to comment. As usual he was expected to save the day. He shifted his weight and guided the Pelnack up into the clouds to make chase.

Kitty stared into the firm black chest of her captor; his feathered cloak flapping like the wings of a raven, his dark eyes emotionless. Glancing below, the Pelnack had disappeared. She tried to wriggle free from Heragus, but his grasp was too strong. "Let me go!" she demanded. "I order you to let me go." Ignoring her, he tightened his grip.

"I said, let me go!" she screamed this time, kicking her legs into his shins and beating at his chest.

"Fine, if that's what you want," replied Heragus calmly, as he freed his grasp.

Kitty dropped into the sky below, spiralling and tumbling towards the ground. She thought of everything that had happened. The friends she had made; the lessons she had learned. It could not end like this because this was not the end of her journey. She knew in her heart that this was only the beginning.

Her thoughts ended with an abrupt thump as Heragus flew alongside her and slipped his arm around her waist, pulling her again towards him. "You are returning to the Regent where you belong," he insisted.

"I wouldn't be so sure of that," commented a voice from below. Kitty felt the whoosh of air as the Pelnack darted in beside them. Iris reached out and grabbed her legs. Yanking at them she yelled, "Let her go you oaf."

Heragus started to spin. Twisting and twirling, he corkscrewed across the sky. Iris's hands broke free as he darted away. "Faster, Vinnie!" she bellowed.

Shooting up after him, the wings of the Pelnack thundered against its side, forcing it onwards and upwards. Kitty's feet in sight, Lilana grabbed a vine from her bag. Looping it over her arm, she flung it as hard as she could. It hooked over Kitty's toes. She wrapped her arms around the leg of the Pelnack and shouted, "Vinnie, head down. Head down!"

Heragus felt a tug on his waist as the Pelnack plummeted towards the ground. Dragging him back and down, Kitty began to slip from his grasp. He tightened his grip as they plunged towards the earth.

Vinnie pulled on the Pelnack's ears, drawing his nose up towards him. The Pelnack slowed to a hover. He watched Heragus and Kitty shoot down, and then swing underneath them on the vine like a pendulum. They shot up into the air, hovering above for a moment before shooting down again towards the forest below. Disorientated, Heragus dropped his prisoner and dived down. Lilana and Iris dragged the vine towards them with a dizzy Kitty attached.

Lilana clutched Kitty's hand, dragging her towards the Pelnack as Iris leaned over the side.

Heragus headed back towards the Pelnack, swooping from side to side. Iris watched as he increased his speed, darting up next to her and then dropping again below. Waiting patiently, she watched and anticipated his next move. Switching sides, she glanced over the edge as he reached up to grab the leg of the Pelnack. It lurched sideways. Iris took her chance, grabbing Lilana's bag.

"Night, night," she waved as she sprinkled a handful of Snorosa pollen into the air and Heragus inhaled. Blinking twice, his eyes darkened, twitched, and slowly closed. She watched the black blur of Heragus tumble to the ground.

Chapter 23: The Final Message

When Kitty awoke, they were still flying. Wrapped in blankets, Lilana and Iris welcomed her back. "How do you feel?" Lilana asked.

"Lucky," replied Kitty as she shivered and rubbed her hands together. "And hungry," she added as her stomach moaned.

Vinnie passed her an oat Crumbler. "We are free," he noted as she nibbled the corner hungrily. "What now?"

"I'm not sure," replied Kitty, rubbing her hands together and blowing on them to warm them up. "I think freedom is enough for now. Let's just get used to that."

"Come on," urged Vinnie, "We've escaped a prison, freed Groggles, saved children from a tyrant... We are on a roll!"

Kitty, still cold from her flight, plunged her hands in her pockets. Confused, she pulled out a folded piece of paper. "It's a note," she muttered, looking surprised.

"Where's that from?" asked Iris.

"I don't know?" Kitty responded, turning it over in her fingers. "It's on Regency paper. One of

204

the Ratlings maybe?" She opened it and began to read.

"What does it say? Who's it from?" Vinnie asked impatiently, as Kitty's eyes darted across the page.

Pausing for a moment, she read the note aloud. "Kitty Midnight, your mother is alive. Find her, and you will find your gift."

Lilana and Iris gasped, open mouthed. They stared as Kitty absorbed the words. Was her mother really alive?

"Well, that answers that question," declared Vinnie, gnawing on an oat Crumbler.

"What question?" Kitty looked up from the note.

"What now?" he repeated. "Clearly the next move is finding your mother!"

Kitty looked out into the darkness wondering what adventure lay in wait. If her mother was alive, then Kitty wanted to find her. Maybe she would be the key to finding out more than just her gift. Maybe she was the key to everything. She could save them all.

She glanced around at her circle of friends, all staring expectantly, awaiting an answer. She ruffled the ears of the Pelnack. "Well... What are we waiting for?!"

....

Coming soon!

The next instalment of Children of the Periapt.

Children of the Periapt: Who is Kitty Midnight?

Sign up for the latest news, competitions and giveaways at www.childrenoftheperiapt.com

And don't forget to leave a review where you purchased.

Printed in Great Britain
by Amazon

61904320R00123